TRUE BLUE

Red Hot & Blue

Cat Johnson

New York Times & USA Today Bestselling Author

ISBN-13: 978-1986837934
ISBN-10: 1986837939

RED HOT & BLUE

Red Blooded
Smalltown Heat
A Few Good Men
Model Soldier (Bonus Edition)
A Prince Among Men
True Blue

BULL

CHAPTER ONE

"Go, go, go!" Jimmy Gordon's shouted command reverberated through the communications implant in Bull Ford's ear.

Following his team leader's order, Bull took off running at full speed.

He'd already scoped out how a nearby rock formation would be the perfect place to take cover. Acutely aware of the location of his backup, the other members of his team, he headed for the shelter of the outcropping.

He flung himself flat on his belly, hidden from view not only by the rocks, but also by the night and the black body armor he wore.

From his position Bull could see his objective—a bomb duct-taped to a live hostage. His task was to disarm the bomb and get the hostage out alive, preferably without getting himself killed in the process.

Knowing its composition would help him in disarming it.

"What info do we have on the bomb?" He'd whispered the question so the targets wouldn't hear.

"Nada. You're on your own."

"Shit." Bull swore softly at the information that came from Matt Coleman, who was manning the communications console.

"Shit is right, Bull." Jack Gordon's cocky southern drawl invaded Bull's earpiece. Jack chuckled. "Get it? *Bull shit*?"

"Shut up, Jack." Jimmy reprimanded his little brother and then asked, "What ya planning, Bull?"

"Do we have a location on the tangos?" Bull answered his team leader's question with one of his own.

Since he knew nothing about the bomb, it would be nice to at least know where the bad guys were.

"I see two targets by the hostage. Two more walking the perimeter," BB Dalton answered.

BB had the best vantage point from his position on the ridge high above the rest of the team.

An idea began to come together in Bull's mind.

"We need a diversion. I'm going to put together a bomb for a phony explosion. It'll look and sound like a real one, but without the kick. Just lots of noise and smoke." As Bull reviewed his plan aloud for the team, he opened the pack he had strapped to his back and pulled out what he needed. "Trey, you have a bead on the hostage?"

"Affirmative," Trey Williams answered.

"Good. When I say three, you fire a few rounds as close to him as you can without hitting him. While the tangos are shooting back at the source of the incoming fire, that being you, I'll lob my fake bomb near the hostage . . ."

"And the tangos will think the hostage was hit by incoming and their own bomb blew," Jimmy finished the sentence for him. "When they run like hell you can complete the rescue. Get him to safety and diffuse the real bomb. Good plan, Bull."

"What's your ETA on the fake bomb?" Trey asked.

"Sixty seconds." Bull reevaluated the timing, his fingers working quick but sure. "Correction. I'm done. Ready, Trey?"

"Affirmative."

"One, two, three."

On *three*, the dirt around the hostage jumped, flying into the air from dozens of tiny percussions. The man taped to the explosives jumped right along with the dirt.

Bull heard him shout a curse as the fake bomb landed within a few feet of him.

It detonated a second later with an explosion of noise and thick black smoke. He felt bad scaring the guy he was supposed to be saving, but there was no way to communicate the plan to him safely.

As anticipated, the tangos took off running away from the explosion.

Bull ran in low. Holding a penlight in his teeth, he shined the beam on the bomb. He whipped out a knife to cut the duct tape so he could remove it from the man.

The hostage's eyes went wide. "Don't. There's a trip wire under the tape. You'll set it off."

Bull sighed. He hated duct tape. He despised homemade bombs even more.

This one looked like the typical homegrown version. The kind you get when the how-to instructions came off the internet, which meant it was unstable and could blow at any moment.

He evaluated what he could see of the bomb and the wires attached to it. With hands as steady as any brain surgeon's, he selected one wire, held his breath and snipped.

When he didn't blow up, he let out the breath.

"Bomb disarmed," he said for the benefit of the team and the hostage.

"Get yourself and that hostage back to home base and we'll call this mission complete. Good job, Bull."

"Thanks, Jimmy." Bull rose on one knee and glanced at the hostage. "Come on. We're outta here."

Bull felt the hit strike his flak jacket directly over his heart.

The force knocked him off balance. He found himself flat on his back, staring up into the face—and the gun—of a grinning black-clad figure. "Not so fast, dog face."

Bull, powerless to help, watched the gun swing to the side and take out the hostage with a single shot.

He closed his eyes and let his head fall back to the ground. "Shit."

CHAPTER TWO

"The plan was good and solid, Bull. Just don't get yourself and the hostage killed next time and it'll be all good. Okay?"

"It's not all good." Bull hung his head, shaking it from side to side. "I fucked up the exercise, Jimmy. You were team leader and I made you look bad. I made the whole damn team look bad. I'm sorry."

Jimmy leaned forward in the red vinyl booth where they sat near the back door of the bar near base. "Somebody had to win. This time, it wasn't us. Next time, it will be. We didn't look bad."

"Bull sure wasn't looking good a little while ago, with that pink crap all over his flak jacket from the paint-ball gun. What kind of man chooses pink paint balls anyway?" Jack asked.

"That dickhead Marine jarhead on Kappa, that's who." Matt scowled. He'd been recruited out of the Army's Delta Force Tech Unit. He glanced at Jack and Jimmy, who'd both been Marines prior to Task Force Zeta. "No offense."

Jimmy raised a brow. "None taken."

"I don't mind losing. Don't get me wrong. In every loss is a lesson that could save our lives next mission, but getting beat by Task Force Kappa? *That's* what really sucks." BB, the Navy SEAL on the team, trailed a finger through the condensation dripping down the side of his glass of soda. He shook his head "We're never going to hear the end of this."

"I know." Bull sighed. "I'm sorry."

"Dammit, stop apologizing." Jimmy slapped his palm against the table. "We're a team. You weren't out there alone. It's as much BB's fault for not seeing the fifth tango on the infrared. Or Matt's for not tracking him on the geo-thermal satellite image. Or any of the guys for not taking out that guy before he took out you and the hostage. And don't forget, we ran this exercise without the commander and down a man because Blake is on leave."

Bull knew all that. It didn't help.

"Jimmy's right, Bull." BB nodded. "I should have seen the fifth tango sneaking up on you and I didn't."

"I guess we all got a little cocky thinking the exercise was over once you disarmed the bomb. We forget it's not over until we're all home safe." Trey's reasoning didn't help Bull feel better.

"Besides that, Bull, you're a really big target. I mean, who could miss ya?" Jack added with a crooked grin.

Not helpful. Bull scowled and took another swig of beer.

Jimmy shot Jack a glare, before turning back to Bull. "Tomorrow morning at the team meeting we'll go over the scenario again with the commander, step by step. We'll ascertain what went wrong and come up with alternate actions we could have taken. What BB said is right. Losing an exercise is more valuable than winning if you learn from your mistakes."

"*We'll ascertain what went wrong.*" Jack laughed. "Jesus, Jimmy. You sounded just like the commander."

Trey grinned at Jack's imitation of his brother. "Before we know it, Jimmy will be taking over the team."

"That ain't gonna happen." Jimmy shook his head.

"Yeah. The commander ain't the type to retire," Jack agreed. "He won't leave until they force him to and he's not that old yet."

"How old is he anyway?" BB asked.

There was a general blank stare and a few shrugs from the men seated around the table.

It was obvious the rest of the team had all moved on from tonight's loss on to other topics of conversation, but Bull couldn't seem to.

He planted his palms on the table and hoisted himself out of his seat. "I'm gonna head out."

Jimmy's gaze tracked Bull as he moved around the table. "You going home?"

"Nah, I think I'll swing by Lana's for a little sexual healing." Bull forced a smile for Jimmy's benefit, before his team leader decided to follow him to make sure he got home okay.

If the team thought he was on his way to his on-again-off-again girlfriend's house to get laid, they'd stop worrying about him.

Hell, maybe he'd even do it. He made that decision amid the calls of encouragement that followed him out the back door that led to where he'd parked.

Heading for Lana's warm bed instead of his own cold, empty one sounded like a damn good idea about now.

Why not? Hell, hadn't he held Lana all night long while she cried when her cat was missing? Surely, she'd reciprocate by cheering him up.

Sinking into her would go far to get him over tonight's disastrous loss. That's what relationships were about, weren't they? Being there for each other.

That and not having to hook up with a stranger when he wanted some loving.

She didn't live too far from base. It only took about five minutes to drive there.

Before he knew it, he was on her block, but there were no parking spaces in front of her house. He pulled his truck up to the curb a few doors down from Lana's and turned off the ignition.

He pulled out the key and sat for a second in the dark. It was late and he was beat.

Both mentally and physically tired, Bull rubbed his hands over his face to wake himself up. He needed a hot shower, some sweaty sex and a good night's sleep. All three could be gotten at Lana's house.

Hopefully, things would look brighter in the morning.

Taking a deep breath, he got out of the truck and locked the door behind him. He cut across the lawn, his long strides taking him to her front door in no time.

He raised his fist, about to knock, when he heard the soft sounds of music and Lana's hot tub jets bubbling on the back deck.

There was an idea he could get behind, even as tired as he was. A nice soak in the hot tub. Perfect. Exactly what he needed.

Imagining how good it would feel to strip naked and slide into the steaming water, he made his way around the side of the house.

He pictured peeling off Lana's bikini and sitting her in his lap. She'd be almost weightless in the water. He could probably guide her up and down his cock with two fingers.

That image had him walking faster.

He reached for the bottom of his black T-shirt as he rounded the corner. He was about to pull his shirt over his head when what he saw stopped him dead in his tracks.

There were two heads bobbing close together right above the waterline. One of them was definitely male, judging by the buzz cut.

They hadn't heard him approaching over the sound of the bubbles and the song playing.

Bull determined that by their matching expressions of shock, mixed with a good bit of fear, when they looked up and saw him towering over them. All six foot four inches of him.

"Entertaining company, Lana?" He noted his voice sounded strangely calm.

Lana's eyes opened wide. "Bull. I thought you'd be gone all night at your training so I, uh, invited a—a friend over."

A naked friend, apparently. Bull took note of the pair of men's shorts and underwear at his feet. He raised an eyebrow as Lana's friend looked ill.

"Really? Why don't you introduce me to your *friend*?" Bull didn't miss how they both remained sunk as low as they could beneath the water without drowning. He'd be willing to bet she was naked too.

With his best imitation of politeness, Bull extended his hand to the turd in the water with Lana.

When the ass took it, Bull pulled until the guy was standing exposed and yup—just as he'd suspected—totally nude and not making a very good show of it either.

Bull dropped the bastard's hand and wiped away the wetness on his black pants.

He shot Lana a look he hoped conveyed all of his disgust.

Sure, they'd had their problems in the past. They'd break up and get back together every couple of months or so. His job and the amount of time he was away didn't help things. But they'd been doing well lately.

At least he'd thought so.

His gaze strayed back to the guy, who probably weighed one-twenty-five soaking wet. Bull outweighed him by a good hundred pounds of solid muscle.

The look on the guy's skinny face proved the asshole realized he was outmatched. He would have been shaking in his boots, if he'd been wearing any.

Bull shook his head. "What the hell are you doing, Lana?"

Still hiding under the water, she turned on the tears while trying to grab his hand.

He didn't know why she was hiding. He'd seen her naked and apparently so had scrawny boy.

"I just get so lonely and you're away all the time."

He frowned at her pitiful excuse. "I haven't been away at all this month." Shaking his head, he realized it just didn't fucking matter. "Forget it."

Bull turned and flung the sliding door that led into her house so hard it crashed along the metal frame, not breaking but sounding close to it.

"What are you going to do?" She sounded a little frantic, but not enough to haul her naked, cheating ass out of the water.

Worried, was she? He snorted out a laugh at that. She'd never even seen him really angry.

She didn't deserve an answer but he gave her one anyway. "I'm getting my stuff.

That's exactly what he did.

He flung open drawers until he found his Army T-shirt and sweatpants. Cabinet doors crashed open as he got his bottle of Wild Turkey—he'd need that when he got home. He pulled open the entertainment center and grabbed his DVDs.

On the way out the front door, he noticed stick boy's tiny sneakers by the door. He kicked at them with his size thirteens. What were these? An eight? Nine, maybe?

Letting out a snort, he bent and picked up the sneakers and walked out Lana's door for the last time.

Cradling his own stuff under one arm, Bull dropped the guy's running shoes down the sewer in the street and hoped they'd been really expensive.

He walked the rest of the way to his truck whistling.

CHAPTER THREE

Marly Spencer's fingers struck an errant harp string. The sound of the dissonant note filled her apartment.

She blew out a breath of frustration. Why did mistakes always sound so much louder than the rest of the piece of music? One of life's great mysteries, she guessed.

The other mystery of the day—and the day was still young yet—was what was she going to do about her gig tonight?

Songs she knew like the back of her hand were coming out sounding like musical torture.

Marly ran her hands over her face. She had to get a grip on herself and stop being so distracted. She needed to focus.

Easier said than done. She sighed and splayed her fingers across the strings one more time just as the phone rang. The way she'd been playing today, it was a welcome interruption.

"Hello?"

"Hi. It's me." The sound of his voice had her heart thudding.

It was him, all right. John. She should have realized that when the caller ID read private number. John was reason number one she was so distracted.

She'd probably never be hired to play anywhere ever again after she messed up tonight's event. She didn't need this call right now.

"I know it's you. What do you want? We discussed

everything last night."

"I love you. I want you back."

How could he sound so sweet? So sincere? It almost made her want to believe him.

Almost.

After all this time, she knew better.

She stood firm, even as her stomach clenched. "No."

"Babe, come on. Let's at least talk about it."

"There's nothing to talk about. Look. I have to go. I have a gig tonight."

"Oh? Where?"

He honestly didn't remember? She could tell by the tone in his voice.

This was typical behavior on his part. Anything that didn't concern him or his family was just white noise. Beneath his notice. That was one of the many things that had made her decide to end it.

They were broken up now, so there was no reason to get angry over his inattentiveness and self-absorption any longer.

"You know where." She sighed. "You and your contacts got me the job."

"Ah, yes. I remember now. Good. I'll see you there then."

"No, you won't—"

"Of course I will, Marly. You said you're playing, and I'll be attending, so I'll see you."

"I know you're on the guest list, but you need to stay away from me tonight. I'm there to work."

It was unfortunate he had to be there at all, but it was unavoidable. His father was a senator and this was a political event.

"Fine, I'll stay away while you're playing. I recommended you and it wouldn't behoove either one of us if you didn't perform well. However, afterward, we will discuss this."

He always tried to order her around. That was yet another cause for the breakup, although not her main motivation.

Oh, no. There was something far bigger and more unforgiveable than his bossy nature and forgetfulness—the steady string of other women he was constantly photographed with by the press.

"No, John. We're done. There's nothing more to talk about."

He was silent for a moment. She knew him well enough to know he was getting angry.

"We'll discuss this tonight, Marly."

She shook her head. He didn't listen to her at all. He never had, and she'd always let him get away with it.

"I've really got to go, John. Goodbye." She disconnected the call and saw her hand was trembling as she held the phone.

Dammit, she was such a sissy.

Under no circumstances could she take him back. There was no doubt she didn't want to, but what if she did anyway?

Why did the thought of being alone scare her so much that she'd settled for whatever little he had been willing to give her all these years?

She wished for the tenth time in as many minutes that she didn't have this job tonight.

If he showed up with sweet talk and promises, she was afraid she might do something crazy in a moment of weakness and take him back.

Facing him was going to be the hardest thing she'd ever done. Right up there with finally having the guts to end it with him last night.

Marly took a deep breath and hated she could hear it shake.

She couldn't worry about him now. She had to work the kinks out of her repertoire and get her dress out for tonight. If she was going to play badly, she had better at least look good doing it.

CHAPTER FOUR

Bull crawled into the team meeting at zero-eight-hundred feeling—and looking he was pretty sure—like absolute shit.

Of all the things he'd wanted and needed the night before, he'd gotten his hot shower, but as for the hot and sweaty sex and good night's sleep? Nope.

After what he'd discovered on his trip to Lana's, neither the sex nor the sleep had been in the cards for him.

He made his way to the coffee pot and poured himself a steaming mug full.

The commander was a coffee addict. So much so he'd had an industrial-sized, restaurant-quality coffee maker put in the meeting room. He'd also instructed each team member to bring in a mug. A real mug.

Bull was just a newbie to the team when the commander told him drinking coffee out of a paper cup—or even worse, Styrofoam—was sacrilege, and he wouldn't put up with any one of his own committing that sin.

The way he felt this morning, Bull would gladly kiss the commander just for the steady supply of coffee alone. Although a little bourbon in his mug would be even better.

Christ. How could Lana's cheating make him feel so damn bad? He hadn't even been in love with her.

Maybe it was that the revelation had hit him on the same night he'd blown the training exercise and let down his team.

These guys, his teammates, he did love, even when they annoyed him. He'd kill or die for any one of them.

Maybe that was what made him feel so crappy—letting down the team and not Lana's straying. That thought made him feel a little better. He refused to think that lying cheater could get to him this badly.

"You look like you had an eventful night." Matt glanced at Bull while pouring himself a cup of coffee.

He wasn't in the mood to talk to anyone about last night, especially not Matt, king of the comments.

Even the man's mug had a smart-assed comment written on it.

The probability of someone watching you is proportional to the stupidity of your action.

Bull usually found the saying funny. Not today.

Matt eyed Bull more closely. "I mean, I'm not surprised you look like you didn't sleep at all, but I would have thought you'd look a little happier after being *up* with Lana all night. No pun intended."

Bull picked up his mug. "Do yourself a favor, Matt. Leave me alone today."

The low tone of warning in Bull's voice wiped the smile off Matt's face. His brows drew low. "You need to talk?"

"No. I need to drink this coffee, get the fuck out of this meeting room and go punch something."

Matt pursed his lips and nodded. "Okay then. Good plan."

Jimmy came out of the inner office, followed closely by their commander, Hank Miller.

Show time. The assembled team took their seats.

The commander walked to the coffee maker and glanced over his shoulder as he refilled his cup. "All right, boys. Before we go over the events of last night's practice exercise, I have an actual assignment to hand out. It's a cakewalk, so I'm putting it out there on a voluntary basis. The gig is solo. No team backup."

Bull raised his hand. "I volunteer."

Trey turned to frown at Bull. "You don't even know what

it is yet."

What the assignment was didn't matter. That he would be busy and away from his team so he wouldn't have to answer questions about his foul mood did.

Bull looked up and found the commander watching him. "It doesn't matter what it is. I'll take it."

"Okay then. It's yours." The commander put his mug down on the table and shuffled through the papers in his hand. He walked to the white board on the wall and grabbed a marker. "Let's go over yesterday."

Bull watched him, and when it was obvious no more information was forthcoming, he interrupted. "Um, sir. Aren't you going to tell me what my assignment is?"

He turned, graying brow raised. "You said it didn't matter."

Bull heard Jack snicker at the other end of the table. He did his best to ignore it. "Yes, sir."

"Don't you worry your head, Bull. I'll tell you where to be and when before tonight. Now, back to the exercise. Somebody hit the lights. Matt, bring up the course layout from yesterday."

The man was the commander for a reason. Besides the free-flowing coffee to keep the troops happy, he'd just effectively taught Bull a valuable lesson. Never volunteer until you're told what the assignment involves.

He stifled a sigh and did his best to concentrate on the review of yesterday's debacle because no matter what Jimmy had said last night at the bar, Bull still took full responsibility for the loss. He deserved whatever this unspecified assignment turned out to be, no matter how bad.

Bull tried to remember that a little later in the morning when he sat opposite the commander in the office and wondered if he'd made a big mistake.

"Excuse me?" Bull hoped he'd heard wrong.

"I asked if you own a tuxedo," the commander repeated himself. His grin didn't bode well.

"No, sir. Just my dress uniform."

"That won't do for this. I'll get you a tux." His gaze swept the expanse of Bull's frame, overflowing the office chair. "I hope the big and tall shop rents them." He picked up a pencil and scribbled something on a pad of paper.

"I'm afraid to ask this, but why do I need a tuxedo?"

The grin widened. "You're going to a party, Bull."

"A party?" Bull groaned. "Do I have to pretend to be a waiter again?"

The last party they'd worked undercover together as a team had entailed them all playing wait staff at a fancy black-tie event for a bunch of rich snobs. Bull was good at many things, but serving hors d'oeuvres off very slippery silver trays wasn't one of them.

"Nope, this time you get to be a guest. That make it sound any more appealing?" the commander asked.

He raised an eyebrow. Hmm. Maybe this mission wouldn't be too bad after all.

Good food, served to him by someone else this time.

Pretty women, hopefully in low-cut dresses.

He remembered Jimmy had met his girlfriend Lia during the now infamous wait-staff assignment. Bull wasn't looking for a girlfriend, especially not in light of recent events, but he wouldn't mind a pretty little thing as a distraction for the night.

This assignment might be exactly what he needed. He couldn't suppress a smile. "Yes, sir. It sounds good. What are the particulars?"

The commander went on to cover the unverified threat against a number of high-profile events across the country, one being tonight's party for some political big wigs.

"Command isn't taking the threat seriously?" Bull asked. That was obvious since he was going in alone with no team backup.

"Not serious enough to devote manpower to it. They consider this right up there with that guy who announced on the internet he'd put dirty bombs in those seven football stadiums. You know the one. This threat has no more validity than that one did in the eyes of the higher ups."

Bull remembered. When they'd found the guy, he'd been some nerd living in his parents' basement who got his thrills by scaring a bunch of innocent people.

"Then why am I going in at all?" Bull frowned.

"Senator Dickson is concerned for—let me see if I remember it right—*the physical safety of himself and that of his son.*" The commander did a pretty accurate imitation of the senator they all loved to hate.

Not only was the politician a dick, a few years ago he was a big proponent of military budget cuts that would have shut down their base.

"I'm going to be a personal body guard for Senator Dickhead?" That idea made the whole thing a whole lot less appealing.

The commander's lips twitched at the nickname. "I'm afraid so."

"Will Jimmy and Lia at least be at this thing too?" Since Jimmy was dating the governor's daughter, and this was a big political thing, maybe they'd be there. Bull could handle the security detail alone, but mentally he might need to vent to Jimmy rather than punch Senator Dickhead in the face if the guy decided to mouth off.

"Nope. Sorry." The commander didn't look all that sorry.

Bull drew in a breath and let it out in a sigh. "All right."

It looked as if he'd be alone in his duties playing Dickhead's date for the night. He could only hope to land himself a pretty party guest as a consolation.

CHAPTER FIVE

Marly had chosen her favorite outfit and taken extra time with her hair and makeup. She told herself it was because she wouldn't be dazzling the party guests with her musical ability in the agitated state she was in.

The reality she didn't want to face was that she dressed up because John would be there.

She didn't know which she dreaded more, having to perform on a night when her heart wasn't in it or seeing her ex.

Dread it or not, she still arrived at the job an hour early, as usual. That way she could carry in the harp and do her last minute tuning without an audience. More times than not, while she tuned the instrument the party staff and management would tell her how beautiful it sounded. She'd smile and thank them, all while thinking they must be tone deaf because tuning, to her at least, was far from melodic and no one should have to hear it.

It was an impressive instrument though. Beautiful to look at and to hear. Hopefully the instrument would dazzle the crowd on its own, because she wasn't going to with her playing. Not with John in the room distracting her.

With a sigh, she rolled the waist of the full, ball gown-length skirt she wore to temporarily shorten it.

She'd modernized the traditional black and white checked taffeta skirt with the addition of a black short-sleeved top that showed just enough cleavage. The combination of the long full skirt and fitted top was demure and sexy at the same time.

Of course, while she had the floor-length skirt hiked up so she could carry the forty-pound harp without tripping over her skirt, it was less attractive.

Meanwhile, she had to keep assuring the more than helpful staff she could manage the instrument alone. It wouldn't be the first time nor the last she'd carry it.

Ground-floor gigs, like tonight, were easy. It was stairs that gave her trouble. The weight of the piece wasn't the issue. Its height—or rather her lack of height—was. The harp was taller than she was, all five-foot of her, plus a few inches more if she added heels.

She'd taken her heels off to carry the instrument inside tonight. She definitely hadn't been looking glamorous upon arrival in the main room, barefooted with her skirt bunched up, when she first spotted the tall hulk of a man in a tuxedo.

He was watching her.

Funny, he was the biggest guy present and the only one who didn't try to wrestle the harp out of her hands and carry it for her.

Interesting. She wasn't sure how she felt about that.

She didn't know who the mystery man was. He wore a tuxedo—vest, bowtie, cufflinks and all—but he was early for a guest and it somehow didn't seem as though he was there for the party.

He wasn't one of the wait staff.

Maybe he was part of a security detail? That would fit, judging by the sheer size of him.

All she did know was that she had better fix herself before any other guests showed up.

She pulled down the skirt to proper length, slipped her shoes back on and then set about divesting the harp of its canvas bag. She threw the harp cover and her big purse in the corner of what was now serving as a storage closet.

It wasn't the first time she'd been hired to entertain here. It was nice being in a familiar venue. She knew where everything was and didn't have to bother the staff.

This mansion was used for more political fundraisers and hoity-toity parties than she could count. The rich may stay at the outrageously overpriced suites at the Hilton in town, but they partied in the historic Lynwood House.

Since it had once belonged to a turn-of-the-century robber baron, she figured parties in the forty thousand square foot house were nothing new. These walls had seen their share of rich people doing all sorts of things over the past century.

Mr. Tall Dark and Serious caught her eye again as she set up her music stand.

He seemed intent on staring at her while still managing to scan the room, before his gaze would come back to her.

Definitely security. Probably Secret Service. Who knew? Maybe the president would show up.

Great. Just what she needed. As if she weren't nervous enough.

She propped up the notebook full of sheet music and turned to adjust her stool. When she glanced his way again, it was to discover that the mysterious man had moved out of the room.

Thank God for small favors. She didn't need him as a distraction too. It was all she could do to concentrate given her dread of the impending confrontation with her ex.

No matter that John had assured her he would leave her alone during the party, there was still *after* the party to worry about.

CHAPTER SIX

"I want you by my side at all times. Do you understand?"

Senator Dickhead was tall, but Bull was taller and wider, so when he stood next to the man for his lecture, he felt like an overgrown child.

"Sir, I'll be far more effective standing apart from you where I can see a threat coming from any direction. If I'm next to you, there will always be a blind spot."

Didn't the man know to trust the professionals?

Bull had learned the hazards of ignoring the blind spot when he'd gotten taken out during last night's exercise. Only anyone shooting at Dickhead tonight wouldn't be using paint balls.

As much of an idiot as the senator was, it was still Bull's job to protect him.

Dickhead considered Bull's point for a moment. "All right. But no farther than ten feet. And when my son arrives, you'll have to keep an eye on both of us."

Oh, joy. Why didn't Bull just get some rope and tie the three of them together?

Jimmy should have been sent with him on this crap assignment. These were his people now that he was living with the governor's daughter. They sure as hell weren't Bull's kind of people.

Not only was Dickhead acting like a dick, but Bull's bowtie was strangling him and his leg holster was starting to chafe his skin beneath his pants leg when he walked.

Fuck this formal wear crap. Give him his flak jacket and an automatic weapon strap over his shoulder any day.

The senator turned and strode from the relative privacy of the foyer where they'd been discussing the safety issue, and into the main room.

As instructed, Bull paced ten feet, rolled his eyes and then followed in Dickhead's wake.

Once in the main room, the older man paused to speak with some rich dude, so Bull stopped and took the opportunity to evaluate the guests.

He thought it doubtful the man and woman Dickhead was currently bending the ear of posed a risk. He doubted anyone invited to this party presented any sort of danger at all, except for maybe boring him to death.

Matt and his magic computer had run an in-depth search on every name on the guest and staff lists. They'd all come up clean as a whistle.

Well, at least as far as security was concerned, they had. He wouldn't be surprised if there were plenty of skeletons in the closets of these folks. It seemed rich people and politicians were on the news every day for some scandal or another. Couldn't keep their dicks in their pants or their hands out of someone else's pocket.

He glanced around the room one more time. There wasn't much else to do except stand here and keep his eyes open. He'd arrived earlier than the guests and swept the building top to bottom for explosives.

If the threat came sometime during the party from outside the building, such as a missile or a car bomb, Bull was helpless to stop it anyway. Especially if he remained tied to the senator on an invisible ten-foot leash.

All he could do was endure his uncomfortable shoes and wait for the unlikely event that the little old man and his much-too-young date speaking with the senator now might whip out a knife and stab Dickhead. Not that Bull could blame them if they did.

Oh, he'd stop them, but he'd definitely understand their motivation.

At least there was one upside to the evening. His gaze swept the room and settled on the cute little thing he'd seen effortlessly hefting a harp bigger than she was.

It had seemed she wouldn't have had any problem at all carrying the instrument if she weren't wearing that ridiculously long skirt.

He did like her top though. Low cut and tight in all the right places. She had the assets to show it off right too.

She played the harp like an angel but had a body built for the devil, just how he liked.

Mmm, mmm. He'd have to volunteer for babysitting duty more often if this scenery came with it.

Maybe after Dickhead left for the night, Bull would help her carry the thing out to her car. She might even thank him with a kiss. Wouldn't that be nice?

"Bull." Matt's voice seemed to explode out of Bull's eardrum.

He jumped and turned toward the wall so the other guests in the room wouldn't see him talking to himself. "Jesus, Matt. You scared the crap out of me. What?"

"The threat's been bumped up. It looks like it's fucking real. We're on our way to you now."

"Where's it coming from?" Bull's heart kicked into high gear as his gaze sought out the senator.

"It's right up your alley, buddy. Chatter on the lines indicates a bomb."

"I swept the building—"

"It's hidden somewhere inside the walls."

"What? How?" Bull had spoken rather loud and got a few stares from the guests nearest him.

"There were workmen there six frigging months ago repairing the plaster. One of them has suspected terrorist ties. I was bored and started to check back just for fun."

Bull never did understand Matt's idea of fun, but it was a damn good thing he'd decided to have some fun tonight.

A work crew six months ago had planted the bomb? This had been in the works for a while. Organization like that meant these guys weren't amateurs.

"Now the original threat makes sense." Matt continued, "It was some sort of riddle about the walls of Jericho coming down. No one took it seriously until I found the record of the crew that worked on the walls."

"What do you want me to do until you get here?" Bull didn't want to start a panic and he really didn't want to tip his hand if there was a triggerman on site.

If the bomb was built to detonate, that trigger device could be held by anyone inside or outside the building. Letting that person know the good guys had discovered the plot would force the bomber's hand.

In light of this new information, Bull reevaluated the guests and staff.

There weren't many people here. It was still early. That was good. The terrorist would want the biggest bang for his buck and wait for a full house.

"Get the senator out, first of all. We'll never live it down if he gets killed on our watch. But don't let him know anything. Don't let *anyone* know anything yet," Matt instructed.

"Roger that." Bull turned away from his corner and surveyed the room. He moved toward the senator, still in conversation right where he'd left him.

"Sir. Excuse me for interrupting. I need to speak with you." When Dickhead—the frigging cocky idiot—looked annoyed that the security he'd insisted on being up his ass all night had bothered him, Bull added, "It's urgent."

It must have hit him something was wrong. His eyes went wide and he opened his mouth.

Bull grabbed his arm and pulled him away from his companion and out of the room before he could blow their one advantage—the element of surprise.

The guests, and probably the terrorist, would guess Bull

was security, but no one but the senator knew he came attached to a special task force highly trained for situations exactly such as this. And no one knew the good guys had discovered what the bad guys were up to.

Outside the building, Bull did a visual sweep of the area. It was deserted except for a few valets waiting around to park any new arrivals' cars.

Even so, Bull pulled the senator to where they could speak without being heard.

"What's happening?" Dickhead's voice rose, tinged with panic.

He didn't feel comfortable telling Dickhead the truth, didn't trust him to keep his cool or keep quiet, so he'd have to make up some cock-and-bull story.

The man was probably a Chicken Little—the type to run around screaming at the slightest provocation. No way Bull could tell him there was very likely a bomb hidden inside the walls of the building where his hoity-toity associates still were.

"Nothing yet." That wasn't exactly a lie. "It's just a precaution."

"If it's nothing, then why the hell did you drag me out here?"

Bull clenched his jaw and mentally talked himself down from telling the senator what he thought about him. "There's new information about the threat. My orders are to keep you out of the building until further notice."

They should evacuate.

The commander would probably have Bull trip the fire alarm. That would clear the building but wouldn't tip off the bombers. But until the commander and the team arrived, his orders had been to get Dickhead out, and he'd done that.

If the senator would just stay put and keep his mouth shut, Bull could go back in and unobtrusively search for the bomb and the bomber . . . if Dickhead would behave and let Bull do his job.

The senator scowled. "What am I supposed to do? Stand out here in the driveway like an idiot?"

He was already doing a good job of being an idiot, so that sounded like a good idea to Bull.

A long black car pulled up and he recognized Dickhead Junior being helped out of the back seat by the driver. "It looks like your son's arrived. I'd strongly advise you and he take the car and go elsewhere until the situation has been reevaluated. Somewhere far."

Like out of the blast zone.

There must have been something in Bull's tone or expression, but the senator quit acting annoyed and started to look concerned. Lucky for Bull, Dickhead was a chicken shit and all in favor of saving his own skin.

"All right. You have my number?"

"Yes, sir."

"Keep me updated."

"Yes, sir." Bull watched Dickhead steer Junior back into the car.

He waited until the vehicle drove off the property, just to be sure. Then he turned on his rented shoe heel and headed for the entrance.

"Matt, Dickhead and Little Dick are off the property. I'm heading back inside to see if I can spot the trigger man or find evidence of the bomb's location."

"Roger that."

"Matt, we've still got civilians inside. Between staff and guests, about two dozen."

"I know, but until I recheck everyone, we can't clear them out. One of them could be our tango."

"Copy." Inside, Bull heard the harpist begin a new song and asked, "Can you check the harpist?"

"Do you think she's our tango?"

"No. Just covering all the bases." He did think it would be a shame if she accidentally got blown up though. Maybe he'd come up with some bogus reason to get her out of there once Matt had cleared her.

"Okay. Give me a few min—shit, Jack! Take it easy on the turns. I almost dumped the laptop on the floor. I'm sorry,

Bull, but I'm doing the best I can in the back of the van with Gordon up there driving like he's on the NASCAR circuit. Hold tight. We'll be there soon. It could still be nothing."

"Should I ask around? Try to find out where the crew worked on the walls? It might give us a clue where to start looking."

There was dead air for a moment and then Matt was back. "The commander says no. Sit tight."

"Roger that." Bull sighed.

The one thing he was not all that good at was waiting and doing nothing.

He glanced around the room again.

The wait staff was comprised of pimply-faced boys. Old men and cleavage-baring women guests, and one petite harpist with reddish brown hair pulled into a surprisingly sexy ponytail rounded out the full complement of those in attendance. He'd bet his life—he was betting his life actually—not one of them was the terrorist.

He'd have to start his search again now that he had the all-important information from Matt to look at the walls. But this time, he'd have to do it so no one, the bomber in particular, would notice.

Bull remembered a closet on the first floor. It apparently used to be a bathroom. The old cast-iron tub and fixtures were disconnected but still there, surrounded now by cardboard boxes and paint cans. It was obvious one wall had been freshly painted. He'd start there.

If he were wrong . . . well, they'd know soon enough.

He slipped into the closet unnoticed and began running his hands over the surface of the wall, looking for any irregularities.

"Bull!"

He jumped one more time. It had to be his being alone, without the team, making him so jumpy.

He blew out a breath. "Copy, Matt. What's happening?"

"There's no record of a harpist on my list."

Aw, crap.

CHAPTER SEVEN

Marly had played for forty-five minutes straight. It was time for a break.

Her back was starting to hurt and she was thirsty. The good news was that her ex had never shown up. Thank God for small miracles.

Her agreement allowed for fifteen minutes off every hour she played. She didn't always take it, but tonight she needed the break.

She leaned the harp away from her and rose from the bench. Her legs were starting to cramp from sitting in the same position without moving for almost an hour. She'd grab her bag out of the closet and take a walk around to stretch her legs.

There was always a bottle of water in the big bag she brought with her to gigs, and an apple and granola bar. Thanks to her nerves about seeing John, she hadn't eaten before she'd left the house. Right now, she could probably down all three items, no problem.

Holding her skirt off the floor with one hand, she worked her way through the slowly thickening crowd.

People always arrived late for these things. She accepted the compliments from the guests she passed and headed for the closet where she'd stashed her bag.

She opened the door and slid her hand along the wall, looking for the light switch.

It was here somewhere, but she'd be damned if she could find it. She went farther into the darkness, using the light coming in from the room behind her to locate the bag she'd left on the floor with her harp cover.

Quicker than she could scream, a hand covered her mouth and the door to the main room slammed shut.

Breathing was nearly impossible as an arm as hard as steel pinned her to a body that felt as wide and unyielding as a brick wall.

She struggled, for all the good it did her, but he held tight. She couldn't see but she figured it had to be a man. Women just weren't built that big and hard.

"What are you looking for, sweetheart?" The deep voice vibrated through her back and into her. He pulled them both to the wall and flipped on the lights with one elbow.

A small, high window interrupted one wall. Reflected in its glass she saw the hulk she'd noticed before.

He spun her around and the hand over her mouth moved and grabbed her chin.

She stared up into blue eyes narrowed in anger. He was big.

She'd dated men who were six feet tall before, her ex John being one of them. Marly had found tall guys tended to like petite women, she didn't know why. Maybe it made them feel even bigger. Who knew? But this guy—he was well over six feet tall.

He was broad too, and from the feel of him it wasn't fat. He was solid muscle.

If he didn't seem to want to crush her with his bare hands, she'd say he was attractive. She was having trouble getting past the murderous expression though. It kind of took away from her admiration of his overall physical appearance.

"I asked you a question." He shook her, his hands clamped tightly around her upper arms.

"I came to get my bag." What the hell was going on?

Did he think she'd come to assassinate whomever he was protecting? It was easy enough to prove she hadn't. There was nothing more dangerous in her bag than her tuning key. She could maybe jab the point of that in somebody's eye, but that's about it.

His gaze moved to her bag on the floor. "Really. Why don't we see what you've got in there?"

He tucked her under one arm and half dragged, half carried her toward the bag. Her feet hardly touched the floor along the way.

With his one free hand, he dumped the contents of the bag onto the canvas harp cover.

She hissed as she watched her brand new forty-dollar electronic tuner spill out onto the floor. "Careful."

His eyes opened wide and he drew in a sharp breath of his own. "I bet you want me to be careful. Shit. Matt, I think I've found the detonator."

"Matt?" What the hell was he talking about? Marly shook her head. "My name's not Matt."

There was a good chance she was being held in a closet by a madman, and all she could think about was if her new tuner was broken. When she got out of this mess, she was seriously going to reevaluate her priorities.

She reached for the device to make sure it was all right, but he didn't let her even get close to it. The brute grabbed her wrist hard enough he would probably leave a bruise.

Her heart beat faster. She was in real danger here. But the bruiser had made one mistake. He'd uncovered her mouth. She intended on taking full advantage of that.

She pulled in a lungful of air and got ready to scream.

He slapped a hand over her mouth, harder than he had the first time. He was so big he covered the entire lower half of her face with one hand. He squeezed her mid-section with his other arm until all the air she had taken in came out of her nose and mouth in a whoosh between his fingers.

"I don't like screaming. Don't try that again." The growl in his voice sent her pulse speeding.

Always nice to know your killer's preferences.

She sincerely hoped she wouldn't offend him if she screamed while he murdered her.

Marly became aware of his impressively large appendage pressing into her lower back.

Maybe murder wasn't what he had in mind.

She made a sound in her throat and pulled her pelvis as far away from him as she could get.

He chuckled, not an encouraging sound. "Don't flatter yourself, sweetheart. It's from the adrenaline. I get a hard-on when I kill people too . . . or even when I diffuse *bombs*."

He said the last word with too much emphasis. She was going to end up blown to bits by this crazy man who got sexually excited by killing people, and he was probably going to rape her first.

Black spots appeared on the edge of her vision. Her last thought was it was better to be unconscious for whatever was about to happen.

CHAPTER EIGHT

"Shit! Matt, do you copy?" Matt hadn't answered Bull when he'd told him about the detonator, and he wasn't answering him now.

In fact, he hadn't heard from Matt since he'd informed him there was no record of the harpist on any list.

She was so damn cute, Bull hadn't wanted to let the fact she wasn't on record make him suspicious, but when she came sneaking into the closet in the dark, searching for the ominous-looking little black gadget, he'd had no choice but to believe she could be the bomber.

A girl who looked this innocent and all-American wouldn't be working alone. Chances were high she'd been recruited by a boyfriend to do this. And if so, where was he now?

Bull needed Matt. "Matt, where the fuck are you?"

Nothing. What did that mean?

Were they maintaining radio silence so the tango couldn't monitor them? If so, no one had bothered to tell him.

Had Matt relocated the equipment and hadn't set up again yet?

What the hell did Bull know? He didn't understand half the magic Matt pulled off with his computers. All he knew was now, more than ever, he wanted to hear that annoying voice in his ear because the possible—probable—tango had either fainted or had pretended to faint in his arms.

He stared at the small black box that she'd been so interested in. He couldn't dissect it while holding her, and he preferred to do any analysis of the device far away from the bomb hidden in the walls anyway. He had to locate the bomb and diffuse it. There could still be a second tango with a backup detonator.

Bull glanced at the seemingly limp body of the girl in his arms and got a view down her ample cleavage. As much as he'd like to be enjoying the weight of her body pressed up against him, he had more important things to do.

Having to hold her was seriously cutting into valuable search time, but he couldn't risk her getting away.

After a quick look around the room, he found the solution.

A minute later he had her trussed, hand and foot, with an industrial-weight extension cord. Looking around for a gag and not finding one, he had a brainstorm and whipped off his bowtie. The damn thing was uncomfortable anyway.

Just as her big green eyes opened wide, he shoved the bow in her mouth and tied it behind her head.

She struggled while he began knocking holes as quietly as he could in the wall with the handle of a broom he had been lucky enough to find.

Sit around and wait for backup? Hell, no.

He'd have the thing located and diffused before the team even got damn communications back in place. And he'd redeem himself and the team for fucking up the training exercise against Kappa at the same time.

"Bull. What's your location?"

Finally.

"About damn time, Matt. I'm in what looks like it used to be a bathroom but is now being used as a closet. First floor. Directly off the main room. I'm dismantling a wall that's been recently plastered, and I think I've got one of the tangos and the detonator."

"What?"

"The harpist who wasn't on the list—"

"Shit, Bull. No. It's not her. Listen to me carefully. That list was incomplete. The tangos are the fucking valet car parkers. They weren't on the list because they're not on the payroll. They work for tips. And I checked with the manager. The harpist works there all the time. She's an independent contractor and gets paid by the individual throwing the party, so she wasn't on the payroll either."

Matt's voice—and that he'd just informed Bull he'd made a huge mistake regarding the harpist—was overshadowed by the sound of automatic weapon fire and screaming from the other room.

"Shots fired," Bull said, automatically.

Things had just gone from bad to worse. Bull already had his weapon out of the leg holster, although next to fucking machine guns, a .40 caliber handgun wasn't going to do him much good.

"Bull, listen to me." The commander's voice replaced Matt's in Bull's ear. "Stay hidden. You're our ace in the hole. The bastards now have hostages as well as a possible hidden bomb, but they don't know you're there, and that's a point for us. Hold for further instructions."

"Yes, sir." Bull kept his voice as low as possible. He crept toward the door, gun out, and peered through the keyhole.

Good thing old doors had big keys and therefore, really big keyholes. It served Bull's purpose. He could see pretty damn well.

Three men had the hostages lined up against the far wall, in perfect position to be mowed down with one burst from the automatic weapon. And the only person Bull had gotten out of the building was Dickhead.

He leaned back on his heels with a sigh, took one more look to make sure all eyes were turned away and then flipped the light switch off.

There was no way to lock it from the inside without the key and if the bastards made the mistake of opening the door, Bull and his one gun wanted darkness and the element of surprise.

He couldn't risk the noise of searching in the wall for the bomb with them right on the other side of the door, so he didn't need the extra illumination for that.

And he really didn't need the light to see that he had scared the crap out of an innocent harp player.

If the situation weren't so dire, he'd be very relieved to know she was as guiltless as she'd originally seemed. Although the chances of his getting the goodnight kiss he'd imagined an hour ago, back when this was still a bullshit babysitting assignment, were probably slim to none now.

The one window—too small to crawl out—allowed in some dim light from the streetlamps outside.

His eyes adjusted to the dark and he made his way silently to where she lay on the floor, bound and gagged. It really wasn't safe to talk, but he had to tell her what was happening.

He sat on the ground and pulled her close.

Gun still out at the ready in his right hand, he used his left to move the hair that had slipped from her ponytail out of his way. He pressed his mouth right up against her ear. "I'm sorry. I know you're not guilty now. The terrorists have taken hostages but they don't know we're here. We're safe for now, but we have to be quiet and stay hidden. Do you understand?"

She nodded. Her hair tickled his cheek.

"I'm going to untie you. You can't make even a sound. Understand?"

She nodded again. He untied the gag but kept his hand close to her mouth. Once he was sure she wasn't going to try to scream again, he was free to start working on her bindings.

He'd tied them well. Too well. In the dark it was taking some time to feel the knots and undo them.

His head was bent low in concentration over one particularly tough knot when she raised her mouth to his ear. "Who are you?"

"Jesus, Bull. Who the hell was that? Her voice just gave me the shivers all the way out here in the van."

Bull didn't answer Matt's nosy question.

The warm air from her mouth had sent a tremor down his spine too. That combined with the fact she was pressed tightly between his legs, drove him wild, along with the scent of her . . . part perfume and part her.

He put his mouth to her ear and resisted the urge to let his tongue run over it. "I'm . . ."

What could he tell her? *I'm a member of a secret elite anti-terrorist task force?*

Nope, couldn't tell her the truth, that was for sure. Just minutes before he'd thought she was a terrorist herself.

"Homeland Security." Matt's solution filtered through Bull's earpiece. Matt was as annoying as he was helpful at times.

"Homeland Security," Bull repeated softly in her ear.

It was a good cover. Everyone knew of the department, but no one really understood all that they did.

She nodded and he forced his concentration back to freeing her. Not an easy thing to do when all the blood was in his cock from the sound of her sultry whisper against his ear.

Finally, the extension cord slipped free.

She rubbed her wrists as if they hurt. Feeling bad, he searched for her feet under the hem of her skirt. Gun still out and held at the ready in his right hand, he began rubbing her ankle where she'd been bound with his left hand.

He heard her breathing change and felt her start to shake. Even before he touched the dampness on her face, he knew she was crying.

"Shh." He abandoned the foot rub and pulled her closer against him. "Don't cry."

"I'm scared."

"I know. I'll protect you." He tightened his hold around her waist.

Damn, she was tiny. He could wrap his arm all the way around her with room to spare on the other side.

He'd always dated big girls, Lana included, figuring they'd make him look smaller. After years of teasing that started way back in middle school, he'd done anything he could to look smaller himself.

His first nickname had been Lurch. He'd hated that fucking name. He didn't mind Bull so much. Maybe because his first commanding officer when he became an Army Ranger had given it to him.

The name stuck through his time on Delta Force, right into his days with Zeta.

She quieted and he realized he didn't even know her name. He was about to ask when yelling followed by another burst of gunfire filled the air.

The woman between his legs yelped. He slapped his hand over her mouth and tightened his grip on his weapon.

"I'm going to look. Stay here." He slid out from behind her and made his way silently to the door.

He peered through the keyhole. No blood, good sign.

The hostages were sitting on the floor now, but no one was lying down or looking dead. The tangos weren't in such good shape though. They seemed to be arguing among themselves. He couldn't hear them, but they were animated enough he could tell there was dissonance in the ranks.

Bull crept back to the girl.

"The hostages are all alive." He'd said it more for Matt's benefit than for hers.

The announcement set off another round of shuddering from his companion.

Shit, he probably should have used a better word than *alive*. It reminded her that the alternative was dead.

He sat with his back against the wall and his gun hand facing toward the door. Reaching out with his left arm, he pulled her back toward him. He'd have felt better if she was sitting behind him, or better yet, hiding inside the old bathtub management had left in here from when this mansion used to be a home and this room had been a bathroom.

But she wasn't going to leave his side. He figured that out when she crawled up against him and practically curled up in a ball in his lap. She buried her head against his chest.

It was really quiet in the room and for the first time he realized how loudly her puffy skirt rustled every time she moved. Before, he had been doing the moving, but with her new fetal position in his lap, she was making a shit load of noise, even with every breath she took.

He lowered his head to hers. "What's your name?"

"Marly."

"Okay, Marly, listen to me. Your skirt is really loud. You have to try not to move."

She froze except for the shaking, which got worse. He'd frightened her. He sighed and leaned his chin on the top of her head. She burrowed closer.

Damn, he hated feeling helpless and he hated there wasn't more he could do to make her feel safe.

For lack of anything else to do, he wrapped his arm around her again.

While he was toying with asking her to take the damn noisy skirt off, his body reacted in a way that had nothing to do with adrenaline this time.

Pressed up against him this way, she wasn't going to miss it either. He was a big man and he came with big parts—another reason he didn't date small girls. He'd probably rip her apart.

Damn, why was he thinking about this with armed gunmen and hostages in the next room? They needed to get out of there and soon.

"Matt. What's the status?"

"Who's Matt?" she asked.

He put one finger over her lips.

"Hang tight, Bull. We're going over blueprints of the building. Don't worry, the FBI hostage negotiator is here talking to the head tango and stalling until we get in place."

That was the plan? What happened to the team's usual mode of operation? Get in, take out the bad guys and get out.

Blueprints and an FBI hostage negotiator? They'd be lucky if the damn tangos didn't blow the bomb in the meantime. This was going to take all night, and Bull had a feeling he was going to have this sweet young thing pressed up against him for the duration of it.

Crap.

CHAPTER NINE

"We're going to die, aren't we?" Marly asked as close to his ear as she could get.

She'd never been more scared in her life. She couldn't stop shaking any more than she could leave this stranger's side.

He moved to press his mouth against her ear. "No, we're not."

The softly spoken words and the warmth of his breath helped somehow. It calmed her in a situation where she'd given up hope of ever being calm again.

"I don't believe you." It was probably horribly dangerous, but she wanted to keep him talking, for her own sanity.

Brushing the hair away from her ear with one hand, he leaned in again. "Why not?"

Maybe it was fear of her impending death, but she decided to tell him the complete truth. "Because you keep talking to yourself and to someone named Matt who isn't really here. It's nice I'm not alone, but you're obviously crazy."

His body shook beneath her and she felt rather than heard him laugh. "Matt is the guy at the other end of the communicator in my ear."

She stiffened. That was really good news. Not just that he wasn't a lunatic, but that the authorities were coming to help them. Then again, maybe he was crazy and making things up.

"So they know we're in here? The police or whoever know about the terrorists?"

"Yes." He hissed the word into her ear, and the warmth of his breath sent a shiver straight through her.

She'd really like this guy to not be crazy. "Let me talk to Matt."

He let out another soft laugh. "You can't."

Uh, huh. Just as she thought. She sighed. Oh, well. Better with a crazy guy than all alone.

He leaned close to her ear again. "You can't hear Matt because the communications device is implanted surgically in my ear. Like a cochlear implant. He can hear you though. He hears whatever I can."

Jeez, Homeland Security had some serious spy stuff going on. "Wow."

He leaned closer. "Matt says to tell you he thinks you're very pretty."

Now she knew he was crazy. "Can Matt see me through your ear too?"

"No, but he popped up your FBI file on his computer."

"I have an FBI file?" That was news. "Why?"

"You work a lot of high-profile events. You've been cleared."

"Wow."

"We shouldn't be talking this much. They could hear."

If they hadn't heard by now, chances are they wouldn't, and she had more questions. She'd just have to ask them more quietly.

She turned toward him, but he held her still.

"Shh. Jesus. Stop moving. Your skirt is too loud."

If she got them both shot over her love of taffeta, she'd feel really shitty. She reached behind her, undid the button and the zipper, braced herself against his shoulder and stood.

She rose, but the skirt remained in a giant puff on the ground. Stepping out of it, she waited for him to slide it to the side. She sat down again in between his open legs. It was close quarters, but they had to be close enough to whisper.

"Better?" she asked.

He swallowed loud enough for her to hear. "Yes."

Squashed against him, she felt pretty much every part of his body in detail, one part in particular. His adrenaline was raised again, and so were her curiosity and interest.

"What's your name?"

"Bull."

Hmm. She had a feeling she knew how he'd gotten that name. "Do you have a wife or a girlfriend?"

Might as well get to know a little bit more about him. She already knew the size and shape of his penis. Hard to miss since it was ground into her at the moment. She could swear she could feel his pulse throbbing through it.

"No."

"You hesitated."

Was he lying? In light of the situation, did it matter? She shouldn't care. They both could be dead any moment.

"We broke up last night," he said.

"Really?" She'd broken up with John last night too. Was this fate putting her in this horrid situation with Bull so they'd find each other? She needed to know more. "Why did you break up?"

"Why are you asking?" He answered her question with a question of his own.

Apparently he was the suspicious type. Probably came with the job.

Fine. She could answer him with the absolute truth. "Because your hard-on is crushed against me. Since I'm pretty sure we're going to die, I'm thinking about taking advantage of it."

That shut him up for a bit. He was silent except for a sharp intake of breath, until he said, "I found her naked in the hot tub with another guy."

"I'm sorry. Are you okay?" Hell of a time for a counseling session, but she thought the poor guy might need to talk.

"Besides the men in the next room with guns? Yeah. I'm fine." Bull had a morbid sense of humor. She liked it. "What about you? Boyfriend?"

"No."

"Why not?"

She guessed fair was fair. "I broke up with him."

"Why?"

"He's a dick." That explained it well enough. She couldn't begin to go into all the many reasons he was a dick here and now. Maybe later, when all this was over.

She realized she liked the thought of seeing Bull again, since he most likely wasn't crazy.

"Marly?" The warmth of Bull's breath as he said her name against her ear had her chest tightening. More than that, parts lower were reacting to his closeness as well.

"Yes?" She swallowed away the dryness in her throat.

All the whispering, tightly pressed bodies and true confessions were getting to her. She couldn't think.

"Were you serious?" Bull hissed the question into her ear, sending another tremor through her.

"Yes. My ex was a total dick." She laid her cheek against the warmth of his and enjoyed the sensation.

"No, I mean about . . ." He swallowed again. "Never mind."

Knowing what he was asking her, she turned to face him and straddled his legs.

Without the skirt, it was much easier to move and a lot less noisy. She took a deep breath and ran her hand down his chest, all the way down to the fly of his pants. She touched the bulge there.

She leaned in and brushed her lips across his cheek on her way to his ear. "You mean was I serious about this?"

A shiver ran through him, strong enough she felt it beneath her. "Yes."

"Why do you ask?" She stroked him through the coarse fabric of the tuxedo pants.

"Because Matt just told me the bombers gave the FBI ten minutes to meet their demands or they're going to detonate the bomb hidden somewhere in this building."

She stopped her hand in mid-motion. "A bomb? Here? Where is it?"

"Shh." He reminded her to be quiet and touched her cheek. "Possibly in this room."

"So go get it and throw it out the window." It was an effort to keep her voice low given this news.

Her idea seemed easy enough. Let it explode outside.

The window wasn't big enough to crawl through, but the bomb should fit. How big could it be? She leaned back from him now, wishing she could see in the dark. Maybe she could help him find the bomb.

He reached out, cupped the back of her head and pulled her toward him. For a brief, crazy moment, she braced for his kiss, but instead he angled his head and aimed for her ear.

"It's not that simple. It's buried in the walls somewhere. If they hear me tearing the wall apart looking for it, they'll either shoot us or detonate the bomb. They want to be martyrs. They don't care if they die too."

"So we're just going to sit here doing nothing and wait to blow up?"

"No. We're going to sit here and wait for the rest of my team to take out the terrorists, save the hostages and come get us."

"And what are the chances of that happening?"

"My team will get us out of here. They're the best there is."

"Bull. Please be honest with me. What are the odds?"

He drew in a deep breath. "Eighty-twenty. Eighty percent we'll make it out of here just fine."

Twenty percent that they'd be blown to bits. And who knew if he was exaggerating to make her feel better. She sat for a second and considered her life and her impending death.

"In that case, yes. I was very serious." Running her hands down his arms, she felt the bulge of his biceps through his tux jacket. When she reached his hands, what she felt made her pause. "You're holding a gun?"

"Yes."

Jeez.

"Just don't shoot me by accident. Okay?" She felt him smile at the comment.

Marly was starting to not like the darkness. To hate it in fact. At first it had made her feel safe, more hidden from the men with machine guns outside the door.

Now, she'd changed her mind. She wanted to at least see the threat that would kill her. But since she couldn't, she did something better. She leaned in and closed her mouth over Bull's.

He drew in a sharp breath at the contact, before he parted his lips and deepened the kiss. He cupped the back of her head with his left hand.

The warmth of his tongue tickled her lips then slipped into her mouth. He kissed her hard and deep until, amazed by it all, she found she had trouble breathing.

After unbuttoning his shirt, she slid her hands inside. She felt the hardness of his chest. The warmth of his skin. The light dusting of hair. "Take off the jacket."

"Can't. If they come in, the white shirt will be too visible. Black is better."

Good to remember. She was in nothing but black tights and a black top now. If she got out of this alive, she should start wearing black to all of her gigs in case this situation ever arose again.

Bull had said the terrorists had given the FBI ten minutes or they'd blow the house. She knew enough about the FBI to know they didn't negotiate with terrorists. At least they didn't give in to their demands. They might be able to stall and pretend to negotiate, but for how long?

Marly nipped at Bull's mouth and then worked her way to his ear. She did what she'd wanted to throughout all their whispering. She brushed the whorls of his ear with her tongue and felt him shudder.

"Bull, make love to—"

He grabbed her hair and covered her mouth before she

could finish the request.

She didn't have to complete the thought. He knew what she wanted. She knew that from the intensity of his kiss. How he possessed her lips.

He wanted this as much as her.

CHAPTER TEN

"Dammit, Bull." Matt's voice was an even more unwelcome intrusion than usual. "I was trying to be polite and ignore this tête-à-tête of yours, but come on. I'm getting pretty damn tired of hearing every guy on this team get laid during ops. We're coming to get you out. Can't you wait? You can do this later."

Bull ignored Matt as best he could while Marly straddled his lap. He ran his free hand down her back to cup her very cute, round little ass.

He wanted to whisper things to her, but Matt would hear. He really wanted to have both of his hands on her, but he had to hold the gun.

Though if the tangos came through the door while he was sunk deep into Marly, how accurate would his aim be? The team had never practiced this particular scenario in training.

He should be paying attention to where the tangos were and what they were doing, but he couldn't bring himself to break away from her lips. To give up what she offered.

Christ, what if they did die and this was his last moment on this earth? He'd rather be in her than pressing his face to a keyhole.

His actions were the exact opposite of what all his training had taught him, yet he couldn't stop himself. He plunged his tongue into her mouth as he thought what it would be like to plunge into her.

She slid her hand inside his pants and grabbed his length, which was more than ready for some action.

Any further thoughts flew out of his head the moment she wrapped her hand around him.

As surreal and ridiculous as the situation seemed, this was really going to happen. And he was going to let it happen and enjoy it too, because although he'd told her the truth—that his team would get them out—one question remained. Would it be a rescue mission or a recovery of their bodies?

Matt's words echoed in his mind. *Ten minutes*. They didn't have much time.

He pushed down the neckline of her top. He pulled her breast out of the confines of her bra and covered one nipple with his mouth.

She drew in a sharp breath and pressed closer, but Bull still couldn't totally turn off his brain.

If the ten minutes expired and the tangos went for the detonator, would it be better to come out of the closet shooting and make a run for it, instead of sitting here and get blown up? But what if the bombers were lying and there was no bomb and Bull came out of the closet, gun blazing?

Most likely, both he and Marly would be shot in his attempt to escape.

That left Bull with one thing he was sure of. He was going to take her now, before all hell broke loose. He tried to wiggle his hand into the waistband of her stockings, but they were so thick and unyielding, he couldn't move. "What the hell are these things you're wearing?"

"Tights."

They were tight, all right.

It was bad enough he was restricted to the use of one hand because of the gun, he at least wanted full range of motion with his free hand. "Take them off."

Of course, that would mean she'd be naked from the waist down when they were either rescued or killed. He considered if that really mattered or not.

"Tear the crotch." Luckily, she had a better solution as she stroked his cock.

That command made him groan.

Now that she'd given him permission, he felt for the seam between her legs and poked through the weave with two fingers. He continued to push until he was inside her warm wetness. She groaned as he pressed deeper.

"Hush, baby. No noise." He had to think that was easier said than done when she unzipped his pants and pulled his erection completely out of his underwear.

She angled it toward her entrance.

"Not yet. You're not ready."

"I'm ready." She panted close to his ear as he stroked her with his fingers. He added a third one, trying to stretch her to accommodate him.

"Believe me. You're not." He smiled at her enthusiasm.

She was already wet, but not wide enough to hold all of him yet. That he could remedy. Bull knew his hands were as good with women as they were with bombs.

At least he'd been told so by more than a few happy females. Curling the fingers inside her, he found her G-spot and applied pressure. He heard her breath catch in her throat. He worked her more and she began to tremble.

Bull added his thumb, circling her at the same time his fingers worked inside.

Marly's breathing became more rapid against his ear.

She was getting close, he could tell even before she started to shudder.

"Oh, God. Bull." She let out a stuttering breath against the ear with his implant.

"Aw, Jesus. Bull, please listen to me. We're almost ready to go in. Please wait to be rescued. Get yourself a nice suite at the Hilton where I don't have to hear it. Hell, I'll even pay for the room," Matt begged in his ear.

"How much time do we have left?" Bull asked. If Matt was going to intrude on this incredibly private moment, he might as well be useful.

"Five minutes and counting," Matt answered his question.

At the same time Marly said, "I don't know. Hurry." Then she stiffened over him. "That guy in your ear can hear us, can't he?"

"Yes. Is that a problem?" He regretfully pulled his fingers from her and immediately missed her warmth. Ready to explode, he was willing to do a little begging if she said it was.

"I can live with it." Her answer made Bull want to cry with joy. She grabbed for him again.

"Hang on one second, baby." Wishful thinking on his part had made him stick one single condom in the inside breast pocket of his tuxedo jacket.

He pulled it out now. He had to put down the gun to do it, but he had himself covered in seconds. "Okay, we're good to go."

She took his cock in one hand and lowered herself over him.

His tip nestled at her entrance. He covered her mouth with his and distracted her with his tongue while he spread her wide. He slipped just the tip inside.

He moved slowly, not even an inch at a time. He'd slide in a little bit, and then back off, before he pushed in deeper.

She stretched to contain him, so tight the struggle was exquisitely agonizing until he filled her completely.

In as far as he was going to get, he guided her hips with his hand, moving her in small circles against him as he ground his pelvis against her with every repetition.

Within a few short moments, she started to shudder. Her breath came in short pants against his neck.

The pleasure built inside him as she tightened her muscles to grip his cock inside her.

The tiniest sound came from her throat as the orgasm broke over her. She pulsed around him. He felt every spasm intimately as she came in one long, powerful, silent orgasm.

Once he was convinced she could stay quiet, he let himself close his eyes and absorb all the sensations assaulting him.

The incredible feel of her body surrounding him. Her muscles massaging his cock in a rhythm that had his balls drawing up tight, ready to release. The heat of her mouth pressed against his shoulder.

The spasms inside her stopped and she stilled in his lap. "You didn't finish."

He shook his head. No he hadn't, but he really wanted to. She rested both hands on his shoulders and started to move up and down his length.

She drew in a sharp breath. "You're huge."

"Dammit, Bull. I hate you, do you know that?" Matt's frustrated comment had Bull smiling until he added, "Two minutes and counting. The team is ready to go in if the FBI can't stall them. Finish what you're doing and stay hidden until we say to move. Don't run out and get yourself killed. That's the commander's order. Copy?"

"Yes." Two more minutes. He wished he could go on like this with her for two more hours. "Faster, baby."

Marly did as he asked. As he felt the pressure building inside him, a tremor passed through her. She clung to his neck as her muscles convulsed again.

This time, he went right along with her. He came deep inside Marly with the only regret being there was a definite chance they'd be dead in two minutes.

"Shit. Bull, take cover! They said they're gonna blow it." At Matt's shout, Bull didn't think twice. He picked up Marly, dumped her into the big old cast-iron bathtub he was more than grateful had remained in the room.

He reached down and pulled the used condom off with a snap, flinging it into a corner before he grabbed her canvas harp cover off the floor. He dove into the tub on top of Marly and had just pulled the cover over them when a deafening explosion rocked the building.

Then there was nothing.

CHAPTER ELEVEN

"Well, well. Lover boy is awake. About time."

Bull's eyelids fluttered open.

The light in the room hurt his head. He finally focused his vision on the figure sitting in a chair next to him. Matt, with a laptop.

Bull frowned. "Why am I in bed?"

Matt put the computer down and leaned forward in the chair. "You're in the hospital, big guy. Do you remember what happened?"

He glanced down and saw the IV taped to his arm.

Realization dawned slowly. He was definitely in the hospital, but he had no memories of why or how.

He drew in a deep breath.

It hurt. He'd felt that particular pain enough times before to know what it meant. Broken ribs, or at least badly bruised.

He forced his brain to function. "The last thing I remember we were about to leave for that night training against Kappa. What happened? Did we get in an accident with the van on the way there or something?"

Matt's eyes opened wider. "Um, not exactly. You know, I think I'll go call the commander. He's going to want to know you're awake."

"You better call Lana too. She'll be worried that I didn't

call after the training."

Matt's brows rose. "All right. I'll take care of all the phone calls. You just lie here and don't worry about a thing. I got it covered."

When Matt left to make the calls, Bull glanced around the room. How long had he been out of it? More importantly, what was the extent of his injuries?

He tried to take a mental inventory, but it seemed as if everything ached. It must have been a hell of an accident, but Matt had looked fine.

Why didn't Bull remember any of it?

He glanced toward the end of the bed. His chart was probably down there somewhere. If he could only reach it.

Lifting his head caused enough pain and dizziness that he let it fall back against the pillow, but in his quest for his chart, he noticed something else.

There was a huge red, white and blue bouquet of flowers on the windowsill and next to it, a card and a small stuffed bull.

He was still squinting, trying to read the card from the distance, when a nurse came in smiling. "How are you feeling?"

"Like I was run over by a truck." As he answered, he realized it was a definite possibility.

The nurse laughed. "Glad to see your sense of humor is working fine."

"How long have I been unconscious?"

"A couple of days. The doctor will be in soon. He'll answer all your questions."

She was about to leave, but Bull wasn't done with her yet.

"Wait. One more thing. Who are the flowers and the stuffed animal from?"

"I'm not sure. I wasn't here when they were delivered. Would you like me to read the cards?"

He was about to nod when he realized it would hurt. "Yes. Please."

She made her way to the window and plucked a small

white card out of the gigantic arrangement.

The damn thing must have cost a fortune. It barely fit on the windowsill. "There is just a signature. It looks like John Dickson III."

Bull frowned. "The senator's son?"

"I'm not sure. Could be." She shrugged. "Do you know him?"

"Not personally, no. What about the other things?"

She picked up the greeting card and opened it. "It says, Bull, I owe you for my life. Get better. I couldn't stand it if I owed you for yours too. Marly." The nurse looked up and smiled. "Your girlfriend?"

"No. I don't know any Marly. That's all it says?"

The nurse glanced down again. "There looks like a phone number written here below the signature." She carried the card to him and he grunted in pain as he raised his arm to take it.

He tried to turn his head to see the side table but decided the effort wasn't worth it. "Do I have a phone?"

"Sure do." The nurse pushed a rolling table with a phone in front of him. "Dial 9 for an outside line."

"Thanks." He raised his hand to dial and grimaced as he did.

"Want me to dial for you?" She smiled her happy nurse smile.

He leaned back heavily against the pillows. "Please."

She dialed and propped the receiver on the pillow against his ear. "I'll give you some privacy." She smiled again and left the room.

Bull listened to the ringing, wondering who Marly could be. Wondering also how he was going to hang up once he was done. He'd just have to grin and bear it, he supposed.

The ringing stopped and a woman's mechanized voice said, "Hi. You've reached Marly. Leave a message and I'll get back to you." That was followed by a beep.

Bull almost got stage fright and hung up. He might have if the phone table didn't seem so far away.

"Um, this is Bull. I just wanted to say thank you for the card." What else could he say? Besides, *sorry I don't remember you*, nothing came to mind, so he wrapped it up. "Thanks again. Bye."

He struggled to get the receiver back in the cradle and then crashed backward, bouncing off the pillow, exhausted from that small effort.

This recovery was going to suck, he could tell already. He only wished he knew what he was recovering from.

CHAPTER TWELVE

Marly arrived home in an emotional funk.

At least the insurance company was going to fork up the cash to replace her harp. That had been an interesting form to fill out.

Cause of damage—terrorist bombing.

That reason had required a bit of explaining.

Luckily, the bombing had been all over the news and the caterers could verify she had been there. Proving the claim to the insurance company shouldn't be a problem.

The problem was her new instrument wouldn't arrive for weeks. Until then, she had to rent a piece of crap from the music school in town.

Harp woes aside, the other issue remained that her ex was practically stalking her. Apparently getting blown up and almost killed had made her even more desirable in John's eyes.

She glanced at her phone and noticed a new voicemail. She sighed. Chances were it was him again.

How many calls would this make? A dozen or so in the past couple of days? She took a deep breath to steel herself and played the message.

The sound of Bull's voice had her going weak in the knees.

He'd called her.

Even better, he was not only alive, he was all right. At least okay enough to make a call.

She hadn't been able to get any information out of anyone about him or his condition.

It was like his very existence was a secret. She'd even had to call in a favor from her ex and have him find out not only Bull's last name, but where to send the card and gift she'd gotten him.

That inquiry had yielded a general address for the local military base only, not Bull's home or where he'd been taken for treatment. She hadn't even been sure her card and gift would be forwarded to him.

She had begun to think she'd never see or hear from him again.

Marly remembered that night. She couldn't forget it. It replayed in her head over and over. Like a nightmare, but it had been reality.

Dazed, in shock and deaf from the ringing in her ears, she'd been wrapped in blankets and taken out of the mansion by emergency crews.

John had been outside, frantic for her safety. The sight of the emergency team taking Bull's limp body away had been enough to send her into hysterics while the ambulance crew checked her for injuries.

Thanks to Bull's quick thinking, she'd walked away from an explosion that should have killed her.

Her ears were still ringing, but she didn't have a scratch on her.

Marly had told everyone within hearing distance how Bull had saved her life, but all John had wanted to do was take her home and comfort her.

She'd let John drive her home—she was too shaken to have driven herself—but she didn't allow him to comfort her in the way he had in mind. Not that night, nor since.

Of course, she couldn't tell her former boyfriend she'd had sex with Bull. Or that she was pretty sure he was the kind of man she could fall in love with, even after having only spent a brief time with him that one night.

It was crazy. She barely knew him. But he had saved her life by covering her with his own body, at great risk to himself.

It didn't matter that it was crazy. She wanted to see him again. Needed to.

She looked at the number of the incoming call. She hit to call back and a helpful operator answered with the name of the hospital.

He had called from the local hospital.

"Hello?" the operator said when Marly failed to say anything.

"Um, hi. What time do your visiting hours end tonight?"

"Nine o'clock."

"Thanks." Marly disconnected.

Now she knew where he was, that's where she was going. She grabbed her purse and flung open the door, only to find her ex-boyfriend, none other than John Dickson III, standing in her way.

"John. I'm sorry. I'm on my way out."

"I see that." He stepped inside anyway.

With a sigh, she closed the door and crossed her arms over her chest. "What do you want?"

He smiled and took a step closer. Running his hands up and down her arms, he lowered his mouth toward hers. "You know what I want."

Marly frowned. "We broke up."

"No." John shook his head. "You broke up. I didn't agree to it."

Was he kidding? Only a Dickson would have the nerve to say something like that.

"Are you nuts? Because it's really starting to sound like you are. Every time I pick up the paper, I see you with that other senator's daughter, and everyone is speculating when you'll get married. And before her, it was the governor's daughter. That redhead. What the hell do you want with me anyway? I'm a lowly musician who barely makes the rent."

"You didn't seem to have a problem with the silly media rumors when we first started dating." John continued to hold her arms. "Remember? You let me wine and dine you. Take you on expensive vacations. Buy you jewelry."

He leaned forward as if he would kiss her.

She pulled back, appalled at his insinuation. "I never asked for or expected gifts or trips or fancy dinners. I'm not a gold digger, John, and I resent you making me sound like one."

John dropped his hold on her with a sigh. "Look, Marly. I'm sorry. I didn't mean it like that. I can't help it if my father's second goal in life, right after making it to the White House, is to marry me off into a powerful southern political family. There's nothing I can do about that. But I do know I'm happy when I'm with you. I want to be with you." He raised his hand again and caressed her cheek. "Both in bed and out of it."

She decided to play along with his delusion. "So what happens to us when you do marry one of Daddy's picks?"

"You'll always be a part of my life. That won't change. We just have to be discreet." He shrugged as if it were no big deal. "My daddy's been with the same woman for over twenty years."

The senator and his wife had been married for thirty-five years so she knew John wasn't talking about his mother. That could only mean that for twenty years, Senator Dickson had been hiding a lover from the public, and from his wife unless she knew and didn't care.

Marly's stomach churned at the thought.

John was willing to place her in the role of long-term mistress without a second thought.

She wanted—she deserved—so much more than that. She wanted a lifetime commitment. She wanted a home and kids. Maybe not this second, but one day. She deserved a man who put her first.

Before all else. Before even himself. Like Bull had.

"I'm truly sorry for you, John." Marly took a step back and

out of his reach.

More than anger, she felt pity. He really was messed up. Maybe growing up in the kind of life he had made it impossible for him to be any other way.

"You think you don't have a choice in how you live, and that's sad for you. But I do have a choice, and I would never be happy being what you're asking me to be." She turned and opened the door, then paused and looked back at him. "Goodbye. Please don't call or try to see me again. Take the jewelry if you want. It's all in the box on the bedroom dresser. You can let yourself out."

Still shaking from the encounter, Marly walked out, leaving him standing in her apartment alone.

He didn't look shocked or saddened. In fact, his expression told her he didn't believe a thing she'd just said. He'd continue to call and drop by, but she felt stronger now. She'd deal with it until he finally got the message, gave up on her and found himself a new sidepiece.

But right now, there was someone she needed to see.

Marly drove way too fast to the hospital. She swung her car into a space in the lot and left it parked crooked in her rush to get inside.

She strode into the lobby, not stopping until she hit the security desk. "I'm looking for Bull Ford's room."

The guard searched the list. Twice. He shook his head. "I'm not finding a Bull Ford."

Probably because it was doubtful Bull was his real first name.

The touch of a hand on her shoulder had her jumping.

"That's all right, Joe. I'll handle this."

She didn't recognize the man who'd spoken. He, however, seemed to know the guard.

"Marly Spencer?" It seemed he knew her as well.

She nodded. "Yes."

He took a few steps back from the desk. She followed. "Nice to meet you in person. I'm Matt Coleman."

He smiled and gave her a cocky, knowing look. She

frowned, trying to place him. She met so many people out on gigs, they often remembered her, but she rarely recalled them.

"I'm sorry, I don't . . ." Then it hit her. She drew in a quick breath and felt her face heat. "*That* Matt? Bull's Matt?"

"Yeah. I'm afraid so." He cringed. While she processed that this man had listened to her and Bull during a very intimate moment, he continued, "We need to talk before you go up and see Bull."

"Is he all right?" All her embarrassment disappeared, replaced by concern.

Matt bobbed his head. "Physically, he's healing. That's not the problem. Marly, he doesn't remember anything about that night."

"You mean the explosion."

"I mean absolutely nothing. Not his being assigned to work security at the party, or the terrorists . . . or you."

For the second time in an hour, Marly felt sick to her stomach. "Maybe once he sees me."

"Maybe." Matt nodded. "Our commander is talking to his doctor now to see how to proceed."

Marly knew how to proceed. She would march right into his room, tell him what they'd shared, throw her arms around him and kiss him until he remembered her. "I want to see him."

Matt grinned. "You don't care what the doctor says, do you?"

"Yes, of course I care and I would never do anything to harm Bull, but . . ."

"But you still want to see him." He was still grinning at her.

She felt her face blush hotter. "Look. I know you heard everything."

"I did. But don't stress too much about it." He let out a snort of a laugh. "Believe it or not, that happens a lot to me. No one else on the team knows about you and Bull. At least, I didn't tell them. But no one else knowing isn't necessarily a good thing. You go up there and as far as everyone else is concerned, you're just the girl he saved that night. That's it. How are you going to explain when you freak out because he doesn't remember you or, you know, what you two did?"

"I'm not planning on freaking out." She wasn't like that. Hadn't she sat quietly in a closet while men with machine guns tried to kill everyone? Besides, she knew once Bull saw her, he'd remember. He had to. She crossed her arms over her chest. "Can you take me to his room now?"

"Yeah. Wait here." Matt went back to the guard and got her a visitor badge as she waited with her heart pounding until she was lightheaded.

They reached the room and found the door open, but the curtain drawn around the bed.

People were in there with Bull. She could hear them talking. Marly stopped in the doorway. Matt stayed behind her in the hall, watching her. She could hear a man with a strong Southern drawl. It sounded like he was retelling the tale of that night.

"So the tangos are fixin' to blow the place. They rigged this bomb with instructions they found on the internet. So yeah, it made a hell of a noise, but it was only powerful enough to blow out the wall in the closet where you were hiding. The blast barely even reached the room where they were. There was no way that thing was taking down a big stone building like that. The damn sprinkler system did the biggest damage. The water ruined all the plaster walls and antiques and crap. The historical society is freaking out."

"But there were no casualties?" The sound of Bull's familiar voice made Marly's pulse beat faster.

"Well, no civilian casualties. Although the docs say you probably saved that harpist's life. If you hadn't thought to throw her in that old bathtub and lay on top of her, she would have been pretty bad off. The hostages out in the main room were all scared shitless but fine. But I can tell you the tangos didn't walk out of there. All three of them were carrying some pretty heavy artillery. Once we hit the room, armed and ready, we had to deal with the situation as we saw fit. You really don't remember anything before the explosion?"

Marly held her breath and waited for Bull's answer.

"Not a damn thing, Jack." Bull laughed. "I wish I did. It sounds like a hell of a night. Hey, did anybody remember to call Lana? She's got to be worried about me."

"Here's the phone, Bull. Want me to dial your girl's number for ya?"

Lana? His girl?

A sob escaped Marly's throat as she pushed past Matt. He ran after her. He tried to grab her arm, but she shook him off.

Rather than wait for the elevator, she barreled down the stairs, all the way down to the lobby and out into the parking lot.

CHAPTER THIRTEEN

"I have one question." Besides why he still couldn't remember a thing after the night of the training exercise with Kappa. "Why the hell is Dickhead's son sending me flowers?" Bull indicated the massive arrangement that blocked half the window.

"Don't know. Maybe he likes you." Jack waggled his eyebrows. "You think he plays on a different team than we do? It would explain why Dickhead Junior didn't do it for Lia and she's with my pea-brained brother instead."

"I heard that." Jimmy came around the curtain. "Hey, Bull. Glad to see you sitting up. And I can answer what my brother here couldn't. It seems the harpist you saved is involved with Dickhead Junior. He was very grateful she didn't come home in pieces, thanks to you."

Things were beginning to make sense. Bull nodded and then wished he hadn't when the pain in his head protested the move. "Thanks for clearing that up. The harpist must be the Marly who sent me the card and the little stuffed bull. Now, one more question. When the hell can I get out of here and get back to work?"

Jack and Jimmy both grinned, looking more like brothers than usual. Bull did notice how neither one answered his question though.

Damn military protocol was going to make him prove he was ready for work, both mentally and physically. He'd rather deal with bombs than military red tape.

"Hey, there." Lana's sultry voice filled the room as she sashayed around the curtain.

Maybe when he would get sprung from the hospital didn't matter all that much. Bull smiled. Nothing better than a girlfriend to kiss your boo-boos and make them go away.

Hell, he didn't hurt that bad. He was healed enough to do more than kissing.

"Howdy, boys." She sent Jack and Jimmy one of her sizzling smiles.

Bull felt his cock start to stir just from being near her. "Thanks for visiting, guys. I'll be seeing you." He couldn't shoo his teammates out of the room fast enough for his liking. He wanted Lana alone.

Jack laughed. "I guess we'll check up on you later."

"Much later," Bull added.

Jimmy chuckled as the two men left the room, but Bull only had eyes for Lana as he noticed how she'd left the top few buttons of her blouse undone.

"I was so worried about you. How are you? You really don't remember a thing that happened?" She crawled onto the mattress next to him.

"Nope." He reached up to grab her head for a kiss.

She pulled back. "Nothing at all?"

The poor thing. She was so concerned about his memory loss, he should comfort her instead of her comforting him. "I remember how good you feel. Now come here and kiss me."

She smiled. "All right."

Once Lana began to work her special magic on him, he'd start to feel better.

~ * ~

Recovery took a hell of a lot longer than Bull would have liked.

He'd wanted to walk out of the hospital the moment he woke up. Pain or no pain.

The damn doctors wouldn't let him go home for almost a week. Something about traumatic brain injury.

The worst part was he wasn't supposed to partake in any strenuous activities for another week after that. That ruled out his two favorite past times—working out with his team and having sex with Lana.

He made it a whole day at home after being released. When he'd decided he'd watched every stupid television show, played as many video games as he could stand and had done the very last crossword puzzle he ever wanted to do, he pulled on his sweatpants and sneakers and headed for Lana's.

She'd visited him in the hospital as often as she could around her work schedule.

When he was sprung and got to go home, she'd brought him food, done his laundry, even cleaned his house. She was behaving like the perfect girlfriend, which was a little strange since she'd never acted like that before.

He had no clue what was up. Maybe him almost getting killed made her appreciate him more.

Whatever the cause, her model behavior was making him start to consider that maybe he was ready for more than just a casual relationship with her.

He'd have to think on that. There was one thing for sure, after over a week of recovery—and celibacy—he was more than ready to get busy with her in the bedroom. Or maybe the hot tub.

He knew he could call her and she'd come over, but he'd had enough of being stuck in his house. After the hospital stay, cabin fever was hitting him hard. He had to get out.

Driving wasn't a strenuous activity. The doctors couldn't complain about that.

Getting up into the truck was another story. Cracked ribs hurt like hell for a long time. No way around that. He'd had them before. He'd deal with them now.

He and Lana would just have to take it easy in bed. He didn't mind the idea of her doing all of the work for a little while until he was back in top shape.

Not one bit.

He pulled up to her house and found a parking space along the curb two houses down from hers.

Gingerly lowering himself out of the truck, he couldn't get over a feeling of déjà vu.

Bull cut across the lawn and knocked on her front door.

They hadn't been dating for all that long, and up to now the time they'd been together had been pretty tumultuous, so they hadn't done the key-exchange thing yet.

Before his injury, he thought they never would. He'd had no interest in taking things further with Lana.

Now, it was a definite possibility.

Lana answered the door wearing her sweetest smile and not much more. He took in her tiny top and shorts and smiled. "Hey, baby. I needed to get out of the house and maybe take a soak in your hot tub. Sorry I didn't call. I knew you'd try to stop me."

"Bull, you know the doctor said—"

"I know what the doctor said." He ignored the reprimand in her tone and pushed passed her into the house. He headed toward the sliding glass back door and paused. "Are you going to join me or am I going to be naked in the hot tub all alone?"

"I guess I'd better come with you, just so you don't accidentally drown." Smiling, she followed him outside onto the back deck.

Something was nagging in the back of Bull's brain as he watched Lana strip out of her clothes and submerge herself down to her chin in the steaming water. But she was naked and willing and he wasn't going to waste his traumatized brain's power trying to figure out riddles.

He sat on the deck chair and reached to untie his shoelace so he could get naked and join her.

One size thirteen hit the wood, followed by the second, landing with a thud.

Bull stared at the sneakers at his feet. He could almost feel his brain working, excavating through gray matter, unearthing something hidden just below the surface.

Like a floodgate had been opened, memories came rushing back. He drew in a sharp breath as a jumble of scenes bombarded him.

He had to sort them out as they hit, hard and fast, one after another. The Kappa team member taking out the hostage during the training exercise while Bull lay on the ground, helpless. Coming to Lana's after the bar for comfort. Finding her naked with skinny dude.

The terrorists at the party and . . . Holy crap, the feel of coming inside Marly just moments before the explosion knocked him out while he shielded her body beneath his in the old tub.

His pulse pounded, blocking out even the noise of the hot tub jets. He felt dizzy.

Lana swam to the side and frowned up at him. "Are you all right?"

He shook his head. "No, I'm not. I . . . um . . . I'm gonna go."

"I knew you were pushing yourself too soon. Do you need me to drive you home?"

Now he remembered her cheating, he didn't want her to do him any favors. He didn't want her anywhere near him.

Hell, she wasn't even worth getting into it with. Why yell or fight about that other guy now when there was only one place he wanted to go. One person he needed to see.

He grabbed his sneakers and shoved his feet back into them again, shaking his head as realization fully hit.

It was no wonder she'd been sweet as pie. She'd gotten quite the reprieve when he lost his memory.

Talk about wiping the slate clean.

If he hadn't remembered, she would have gotten away with it. And how long would it have been until she got bored waiting for Bull to get back from a mission and got tempted by another guy again?

They could have started living together. They could have gotten married. That was frightening.

Things were still jumbled and hazy. There were big holes in his memories and missing time.

He remembered hearing something important in the hospital, but he hadn't paid much attention to it then. Now he reviewed it all. Had Jimmy told him Marly was dating Dickhead's son? Yet she'd had sex with Bull the night of the bombing.

The fear of death did strange things to people. Chances were that was why she'd been with him. And she was probably with her boyfriend now. That thought really sucked.

Bull drove toward home but when he got there, he didn't get out of the truck. He sat with the engine idling, not knowing what to do.

He felt like crawling out of his own skin. Like there wasn't enough room for him inside his body along with all the memories. He'd thought he'd be happy his memory was back, but damn, maybe he was happier before, when he'd been blissfully ignorant.

He threw the truck into gear. He needed to drive. Move around. Sitting still would make him crazy.

Bull drove for a bit until he realized he was in front of Matt's house.

Matt—the only other person who knew what had really happened that night with Marly in the closet.

He parked behind Matt's vehicle and headed for the house. He knocked until his knuckles stung.

When Matt opened the door, Bull didn't wait for him to say hello. "I remember."

"Good. About time." Matt took a step back. "Come in and sit down. You look like hell."

"I feel like hell. I remembered that before I got blown to shit, I caught Lana cheating on me. But because I couldn't remember, she was going on like nothing happened. She would never have told me."

"That sucks, dude." Matt shook his head. "What made you remember?"

"Watching her get into the hot tub."

Matt hissed in a breath. "Ouch. Exactly where you found her with that guy."

"Wait. You know? How do you know?"

"You're still running a little slow, I see. I heard everything you said to Marly. Remember? Believe me, I would rather not have."

"Things are still a little fuzzy about that night. I knew you heard the . . . uh, stuff that happened, but I forgot you would have heard me telling her about Lana too. Hell, I forgot even telling her about Lana's cheating. Hey, what the fuck?" Bull frowned at his supposed friend. "You know and don't tell me I don't remember I caught my girl cheating on me? What if I asked her to move in or marry me or something?"

"I thought about telling you, but the doctor said your memory would likely come back in a few days." Matt shrugged. "I would have said something if it came to keys or rings. I swear, Bull. But hey, now you remember you can go see Marly."

Bull scowled. "She's with Dickhead Junior. Didn't you see the gigantic bouquet he sent me for saving her life? I guess she only wanted to be with me that night because she thought we were going to die."

Matt frowned and shook his head. "You really don't have all your memories back yet. Don't you remember that night she told you she broke up with her boyfriend? She called him a dick. Twice."

"Really?" Bull wanted to believe it was true. And since Matt had no reason to lie, it must be. "Wow, I'd never thought I'd ever say this, but thank God you were there eavesdropping. At least you know what happened since I can't seem to remember."

"You will. In time." Matt slapped him on the shoulder. "There's one more thing you need to know."

Bull was afraid to ask. "What?"

"You weren't just a one-night thing for Marly. She came to see you at the hospital the day you woke up."

"She did?"

"Yeah, but she didn't get past the doorway because she heard you inside talking about your girlfriend, Lana. She ran out of there in tears. I tried to stop her, but she's quick for a little thing, and she obviously didn't want to be stopped."

Bull sat up a little straighter and winced when his ribs protested. "So you really think they're not together? Marly and Dickhead Junior? Maybe they got back together after the bombing."

"Doubtful, but even if they did, you're gonna let Dickhead Junior stand in your way after all that happened between you and Marly?"

"Hell, no." Bull stood and then sat again.

"What's wrong?"

"I don't know where she lives." And he'd be damned if he knew where the card with her phone number written in it had ended up. With his luck, Lana had probably tossed it in the trash.

"I got it covered." Matt rolled his eyes. He made his way to one of the three computers set up on a six-foot-long table and started tapping keys. "You want her date of birth, social security number and last year's tax return too?" He glanced over his shoulder and grinned.

"Just an address is good. Actually birthday too, if you've got it."

When they started dating, he could surprise her by knowing her birthday. That would impress her.

Bull laughed at himself. He already had them dating in his mind. He only hoped it wasn't wishful thinking.

In two minutes, Matt returned to Bull and handed him a yellow sticky note.

In Matt's scrawl, Bull saw an address, phone number and a date. February 14th. Her birthday was on Valentine's Day. If that wasn't a sign, he didn't know what was.

"Thanks, Matt. I owe you."

"For that little bit of information? Nah, you don't owe me for that. For making me listen to yet another one of my teammates have sex? Yeah. You owe me big time for that one. *Oh, Bull. You're so huge.*" After the unflattering imitation of Marly that had Bull's face heating, Matt grinned. "Go on, Bull. Go get her. She's waited too long already for you to remember her."

CHAPTER FOURTEEN

Marly's fingers flew over the strings as she completed the complicated piece flawlessly. She should be playing perfectly. She had nothing else to do but practice.

That and mourn the loss of Bull. Although, she supposed she never really had him. She couldn't lose what she never had.

They were together for about an hour during which they both believed they were going to die. That didn't exactly make a strong basis for a relationship.

It was sad that a terrorist attack had been the biggest, possibly the best, thing to happen to her lately, thanks to Bull. Even sadder he didn't remember and she'd never see him again.

She sighed.

Maybe if she'd been the type who typically had one-night stands, she wouldn't be taking this so hard.

Falling for a guy she knew for one night was ridiculous. She knew that, but it didn't help her bruised heart one bit.

The doorbell rang and she jumped. She'd been on edge a lot lately. She supposed getting blown up did that to a person. Hopefully it would go away like the ringing in her ears had. Maybe she could find a bomb-survivors support group on the internet.

Marly rose from the harp stool and went to the door. By standing on tiptoe, she could just see through the peephole, but all she saw there was a broad swath of gray sweatshirt.

Whoever was there was tall. *Very* tall.

Heart pounding, she flipped the lock as fast as her fingers could work and flung open the door.

"Bull." Tears filled her eyes just from the sight of him standing in her doorway.

He stepped forward and brushed her cheek with one big mitt of a hand. She leaned her face against his palm and closed her eyes.

"Marly." He sighed. "I'm so sorry I didn't remember you when I woke up."

"You remember me now?"

He raised his other hand and cradled her face. "I remember you now."

"And what we did?" she asked, afraid to hope.

"And what we did." He leaned down and stopped just short of her lips. "Do you forgive me for not remembering before?"

One tear rolled down her cheek. "Yes. Of course."

"Good." A small smile touched his lips before he closed the distance and kissed her.

She kissed him back, crying and unbelievably happy at the same time. He lifted her off the floor until she was level with him.

He pulled back from the kiss but didn't set her down. "You're not still dating John Dickson, are you?"

Marly frowned. "No. Why?"

Bull smiled. "Just wondering if I had any competition to worry about."

"John's no competition for you. Believe me." She laughed through her tears.

"Good. Because I'd really like to get to know you better." His sweet words made her heart speed.

"The bedroom's right through that door."

He laughed. "We can start there. But I intend to spend as

much time as I need to learn everything I can about you. Your favorite food and TV show and what your childhood was like . . . All of it. You okay with that?"

"Definitely." She wanted to get to know him better too. That thought made her realize something. "Hey, I don't even know your real name. I'm pretty sure your mother didn't name you Bull when you were born."

Was she imagining it or was he blushing. "What? What's wrong?"

"Nothing. It's just I don't like my real name."

"Why not? What is it?"

"Gerald." Bull rolled his eyes.

"So, that's not so bad. What's wrong with . . . Oh, Gerald Ford. Like the former president." Her lips twitched as she figured it out.

Bull began carrying her toward the bedroom. "My mother was a big fan of politics."

"It could be worse I suppose."

"Like how?"

"Well, at least she didn't come up with something like Nixon Ford for the presidential ticket. Or Millhouse for Nixon's middle name. Good thing you're so big. You could have defended yourself when kids beat you up over that name."

Ducking through the doorway, he shook his head. "Yeah, yeah. Get it all out of your system now before we get into that bed. Because I intend to remind you how big I am." He whispered the last part against her ear, flooding her with memories of their one night together.

She remembered everything about him. The feel of his hands on her. The way he shook with the effort to be silent as he loved her. And yes, how big he was.

With his arms still holding her up, she wrapped her legs around his back.

"I'm looking forward to it." Marly covered his face with kisses and then remembered the injuries that had put him in the hospital. "Are you sure you're okay enough for this? You aren't still hurt?"

"Hurt? Nah, I never felt better." He laid her on the bed and then straightened to toe off one sneaker. His gaze met hers and he grinned. "Get naked and I'll prove it to you."

"My pleasure. You get naked too."

"Try and stop me." Bull laughed. As if to prove the point, he pulled the sweatshirt over his head, leaving him in nothing but a tight black T-shirt. "I'll have to go home and change before our date tonight though."

"We have a date?" she asked.

"Yup. The first of many. Unless you've got something else to do tonight. Do you?"

"No." She smiled.

"Good." He pushed his pants down his legs and watched her as she pulled off her shirt. "Oh and Marly. Don't wear tights when we go out. You know, in case I decide I can't keep my hands off you in the truck on the way to the restaurant."

He was obviously used to being in charge. In this particular situation, Marly didn't mind that one bit.

"All right. I'll remember that when I get dressed."

"Good." Naked now, all of the magnificence that was Bull crawled onto the bed toward her.

Finally, she got to see everything she'd missed while in the dark that night of the bombing. It was all well worth shining a light on.

But as magnificent as Bull was on the outside, it was what was inside that had won her heart.

MATT

CHAPTER ONE

Matt Coleman had the best state-of-the-art computer and the fastest internet connection available to mankind. He should. Computers were his life—and that was the problem.

None of that speed and technology made time pass any faster while he tapped his bare foot on the carpet in his living room.

He waited for what felt like an eternity during the long seconds it took the browser to load the page.

When his brand spanking new Matchmakers Unlimited profile loaded, he let out a long, slow whistle. Fifty-four views of his page and more than a dozen email responses and he'd only signed up for the account yesterday.

That number had to prove single women were out there and they were interested in him. It was nice to have confirmation. The way his life had been going, he'd begun to wonder.

Heart racing over the potential buffet of eligible females who wanted him, Matt opened the first email. He leaned closer to the screen just as his doorbell rang.

Crap. Whoever was at his door had shitty timing.

He considered pretending he wasn't home, but his vehicle was in the driveway and the table lamp was on. Uninvited or not, whoever was here would know he was inside.

With an annoyed huff, he took one last glance at the message he longed to read and headed for the door.

Even if Matt hadn't been a card-carrying member of Mensa, he could have guessed who stood on the other side of the door's frosted glass window. He didn't have to be a genius to know it was his teammate Bull Ford. The height and bulk of the shadow was a dead giveaway.

Matt swung open the door wide.

"Hey, Bull. Come on in." As he spoke, Matt turned and headed back to the computer and the lure of his inbox.

Bull could show himself in. Matt spent enough time with the guys on his team in life, death and other much too intimate situations that he didn't need to stand on ceremony with any of them.

"Hey, what's up?" Bull closed the door behind himself and followed Matt into the living room.

Sparing Bull the briefest of glances, Matt sat in the rolling chair and wheeled closer to the computer on the table. "Not much. What's up with you?"

"Marly is working tonight so I thought I'd stop by." Bull eased his massive frame down onto the sofa.

"At least you have a girlfriend." Matt let out a snort. "If you think you're getting any sympathy from me that you're alone for one night because Marly has to work, you're nuts."

Matt was alone every damn night when the team wasn't on a mission or he didn't go hang out at the bar. Which is exactly why he'd turned to his last resort—an online dating site.

Desperate times called for desperate measures.

He'd signed up, but there was no way he could ever let the guys on the team know. They'd tease him to no end.

If he didn't want Bull to know what he'd done, Matt was going to have to wait to read the messages sitting in his inbox and taunting him like the aroma of a sizzling steak to a starving man.

Resigned that he'd have to wait until later, he turned

toward his guest. "So what are your plans for the night?"

"Besides this? I got none." The size of the sigh Bull let out was as big as Matt would expect from the hulking man, though Bull was generally a happy guy.

"What's wrong? You don't seem your usual happy-go-lucky self." Matt figured a man who got to have sex on a regular basis, the way he was sure Bull had with Marly, had nothing to be depressed about.

"This light duty is killing me."

Ah. There it was.

They all went through it—withdrawal. It happened to the best of the men on the team when, for one reason or another, doctors or command kept them from what they loved best—the mission.

"Did they say when you'll be allowed back?"

"They said *soon*." An unhappy scowl settled on Bull's face.

A man like Bull would need a definite, precise date to keep his sanity. Waiting was so much easier when there was an end goal to work toward. Unfortunately, when it came to providing dates, the last thing the military tended to be was definite or precise.

Maybe it was Bull's hangdog expression, or some sort of temporary insanity on Matt's part, but he decided a distraction might cheer up his friend. "If you swear not to tell another living soul, I'll let you in on a little secret project I've got going."

"A mission?" Bull's spirits lifted before Matt's eyes.

"No, it's personal. Online. I was just about to get into it when you knocked." Matt hooked a thumb at the computer, wondering what the hell had gotten into him that he was willing to risk all sorts of teasing just to cheer up Bull.

"Good enough. I'll take anything." Bull planted a hand on the sofa's arm and hoisted himself up with a grunt.

It hadn't been that long since Matt had visited Bull in the hospital after one of their missions had blown up—literally.

Matt would bet Bull's body was still sore as shit. It was

good the command had kept him on light duty, whether Bull wanted to believe that or not.

"What is this?" Bull looked over Matt's shoulder at the screen.

"Swear you won't tell the team?" A little late to be asking but . . .

Bull rolled his yes. "Yes, I swear. Jesus, as if you don't have all sorts of secrets on me?"

Since that was very true, Matt nodded and clicked open the first message. "I opened a profile on a dating site to meet women."

"Really." Bull's brows rose. "And? Anyone good?"

"I don't know yet. This is my first batch of responses."

"Well, what the hell are you waiting for? Open them up. Read 'em to me. Are there pictures?"

Bull really was desperate for some action if Matt's dating profile got him so excited, but at least he wasn't giving Matt any shit about it.

Since Matt was dying to read the messages himself, he was happy to comply with Bull's order and opened the first one. "The profiles have pictures. We can go there after I read the message."

Heart fluttering, Matt cleared his throat and dove in.

"'Hey there, sweetie. Your cute'—you're is spelled incorrectly, FYI." Matt pointed that out, even though Bull was standing right behind him reading over his shoulder. "—'I'd love to connect with you. Hottie57'."

"Wow. She sounds hot." Bull seemed impressed, in spite of Hottie57's blatant abuse of the written word.

"Yeah, I guess." Could Matt date a woman who misused the word *your* for *you're*?

Maybe it was just a typo. A slip because she was so eager to get her message sent to him.

Hottie57 sounded nice enough. Sweet. Friendly. Complimentary. If she was really a hottie, Matt could overlook the typo. And this was the first message he'd read.

Wouldn't it be amazing if Matt found the love of his life in the first response to his online profile?

Sure, it seemed the odds would be against that, but still, stranger things had happened. In his line of work, Matt had seen the long shot pan out.

"Look up her picture." Bull nudged Matt's shoulder with his elbow.

"All right." Armed with the belief that miracles did happen and that Hottie57 could be the future Mrs. Coleman, Matt set fingers to keys and clicked over to her profile on the website.

Her page opened fast enough . . . and his high hopes came to a screeching halt. "Nope. No good."

"Why not?" Bull asked.

"Listen to this." Matt read the details to Bull. Hottie57 was, coincidentally, fifty-seven years old.

"So what?" Bull shrugged. "A little older isn't so bad. Some mature women are sexy as hell."

"Yeah, a *little* older I could deal with. Bull, I'm thirty. That's a twenty-seven year difference." That seemed pretty huge to Matt.

"Hey, cougars are the hot thing now. In Hollywood all you see is older women with younger men. Hell, BB's wife is an older woman and he seems plenty happy."

"BB's wife is only twelve years older than him." But, yes, Matt would agree that BB had never been happier.

Based on that, Matt decided he'd place the limit at a twelve-year age difference in either direction for any woman he dated. That seemed fair.

It wasn't like he was an ageist. Not at all, but he at least wanted a woman from the same generation he was in. One younger than his mother would be nice.

"Anyway, there's like a dozen more here. I'm moving to the next one." Matt deleted the message.

"All right. Fine," Bull agreed—not that it mattered.

Matt opened the next one. It didn't look any better. "Uh,

oh."

"What?" Bull leaned lower.

Matt glanced at his friend. "This one's from somebody with the screen name *Don't Ask Don't Tell.*"

"Hmm." A deep frown furrowed Bull's brow.

Matt had spent a decade in the military. First in the Army, and now in the SpecOps with Task Force Zeta.

He was well aware of the phrase and its reference to the military's former stance on gays in service.

Live and let live was Matt's personal motto, but as far as his own love life, his taste ran strictly to females.

"It could be a girl who's new to this country or just didn't know what that means. Won't hurt to take a look at the profile. Right?" Bull shrugged.

Sure, it wouldn't hurt Bull. Matt noticed how willing his teammate was to send him out on questionable dates, while Bull himself had a nice girl of his own to go home to.

But maybe the screen name was just an accidental reference. Who knew? Giving her the benefit of the doubt, he clicked over to the profile and stared at the picture.

He enlarged it, blowing it up to maximum size, and stared some more.

"Nope. It's a guy." It didn't matter how long or close he looked, there was a definite Adam's apple in the photo.

"No way. You think so?" Bull was too damn tall to see the picture well enough.

"Yeah." Matt slid his chair over so Bull could get a better view.

Bull read aloud, "'Six-foot tall, athletically built. Looking forward to great changes in life soon.' Okay, you're right. Next."

Matt sighed and deleted that message too.

Under Bull's close supervision, Matt worked his way through all of the emails.

By the end he came up with two viable candidates.

The team wasn't expecting any assignments for the next

few days, so Matt responded to both, asking one if she wanted to meet for drinks on Friday night, and asking the other for Saturday. He figured that would double his odds of meeting the woman for him.

When the last email was sent, Matt leaned back in his chair. "That's it then. We'll see if I get responses from the two I asked out."

"How many were there to start with?" Bull asked.

"Thirteen." And only two seemingly normal, single, interesting women of the right age and sex out of the whole bunch. Matt did the calculation. That represented approximately fifteen percent of today's responses.

He didn't know what the site's average was for successful match-ups, but at least one of those two dates would have to be with someone he would want to see again. Right?

Besides, two dates in one weekend was two more than Matt had been on in months.

"Two out of thirteen." Bull whistled, long and low. "I'm glad I met Marly the old-fashioned way."

Matt let out a snort. "If you really believe getting blown up during a hostage situation is the old-fashioned way, you better go back to Medical and get your head rechecked."

"You know what I mean. We met live and in person. Not through this online crap."

Online crap. Matt cocked up one brow. "Thanks."

"Don't be like that. I'm saying this way is fine for you. You're a computer guy. I'm more hands-on."

"Yeah, I know. Believe me. I know." Matt had been witness to far too much of his teammates' *hands-on* activities.

Trey. Jimmy. Bull. The list was getting short of the guys Matt *hadn't* heard getting it on over the comm.

Bull shook his head. "You ever going to stop throwing that in my face?"

"What? That while I was coordinating the team going in to save you and a roomful of hostages, I had to listen to you having sex? Um, no. Probably not."

Bull's lips twisted. "I was pretty sure I was going to die, so get over it. You would have done the same damn thing if the situations had been reversed."

That was the problem. The situations were never reversed, because on most ops Matt's job was to stay in the van running the equipment.

Yeah, his job and his skills were as valuable to the team as any of the others, but sometimes it was frustrating as hell.

"I'm gonna go." Bull turned for the door.

The sudden decision had Matt frowning. "Don't be pissed. I'm sorry. I won't bring it up again."

Halfway to the front door, Bull stopped mid-step and turned back. "It's not that. What the fuck, Matt? I'm a big boy. You know I can handle a little teasing. It's just that Marly is working at another public event tonight. I figure I can pop in and make sure everything is okay."

Understanding dawned. Talking about the mission had gotten Bull antsy. Bull's broken ribs would mend, his hard head should heal, but Matt had a feeling Bull would never completely get over that he'd failed to prevent the explosion.

Even though none of the civilians had been seriously injured, failure was a hard pill to swallow for Bull.

"All right, brother. Say hello to Marly for me."

"Will do." Hand on the doorknob, Bull grinned. "You have fun with your project."

"Yeah, thanks."

As the door closed behind his friend, Matt envied him.

Sighing, he logged out of his Matchmakers account. He was just deciding what need to fulfill first, dinner or a shower, when an instant message window popped onto his screen.

Sam_I_am: *Hey, big guy!*

Matt couldn't help but smile. Sam Foster, a fellow computer and communications guru, always had that effect on him. Matt typed in a response.

Computer_God: *Dude! What up? You need my computer expertise to bail you out of a jam again?*

For the past six months, Sam had held the same position on Omega team that Matt did on Zeta.

They'd never worked together in person, but he and Sam shared information online all the time. Omega team was based out of Virginia, while Zeta was in North Carolina, so the teams didn't cross paths too often.

Matt loved the world of cyberspace. No matter how great the distance, he could still instant message or email when he wanted to bust Sam's chops.

Sam_I_am: *Ha ha! And no, smart ass. I'm pulling an all-nighter. Surveillance. Bored as hell so I figured I'd bother you. What are you doing?*

Computer_God: *Bored at home. No action here. But looks like I could have 2 dates this weekend.*

Sam_I_am: *Been a long time. Hope you haven't forgotten how.*

Computer_God: *Ha ha! Very funny. Thanks for the confidence.*

Sam_I_am: *Shit. Action. Gotta go. Later.*

Matt typed in *Later* and sighed.

At least Sam was getting some action. Meanwhile, wallowing in his sorrow looked like it would be the only thing on Matt's agenda for the evening.

He pushed his chair back from the computer just as an email popped up. It was a response from one of his two dates, WickedWoman.

That was more like it. Action of the romantic variety would definitely take his mind off the lack of action with the team.

Matt clicked to open the email and leaned toward the computer, rubbing his hands together in anticipation.

WickedWoman had written she was up for the date and excited to meet him.

Oh, yeah. So was he.

Hopefully by this time tomorrow night, he'd be getting cozy with WickedWoman.

Even her user name had potential, and her picture—phew. Matt had never seen a woman built like that who wasn't wearing a G-string stuffed with dollar bills.

Of course, he'd give BabyGirl her fair chance too. Who knew? BabyGirl might give WickedWoman a run for her money. Sometimes the ones who seemed the most sweet and innocent turned out pretty wild.

Matt looked forward to finding out.

CHAPTER TWO

WickedWoman was really Wanda, as Matt would come to know after meeting her at the bar inside his favorite restaurant Friday night.

She sipped at her drink. She'd ordered a cosmopolitan, which was basically a glassful of booze with a touch of cranberry to tinge it pink. "So, Matt, what do you do?"

Matt swallowed a mouthful of his own beer and contemplated his answer to her question.

Had Wanda actually looked like her profile picture, he might have considered dancing along the edge of the rules and hinted at his SpecOp status.

However, Wanda's online photo had been taken at least ten years and fifty pounds ago. Oh, the stripper-worthy boobs were still present and even larger than pictured, but the age she'd written on her profile?

Nuh, uh.

Matt didn't mind a curvy girl one bit. Nor did he mind an older woman. But in this lighting, sitting as closely to Wanda as he was, he could see the crow's feet under the caked-on makeup, proving she'd not only uploaded an old photo, she'd also lied about her age.

Her lack of honesty bothered him.

How could a guy trust a woman who lied from the

moment he met her? Any hopes Matt might have had for a relationship with Wanda had been squashed the moment he realized he'd been duped, and that decided his answer to her question.

"I'm in the Army."

"Oh." Her smile faded. A frown knit her brow beneath the makeup. "That doesn't pay very well, does it?"

"Nope." That wasn't a lie. Army pay for the starting rank of private was crap. He just didn't elaborate he was nowhere near that pay grade.

He could see her hopes falling. If she was looking for a sugar daddy, it wasn't going to be him.

"So what do you do in the military?"

"I'm in technology." There, that was the truth. Matt felt a little better not having to lie to that question.

"Oh, technology. That's sounds important." She looked a bit too impressed by his answer for Matt's liking. "Are you an officer?"

Wanda obviously had the good old *Officer and a Gentleman* fantasy in mind. She was probably envisioning Matt in his dress uniform sweeping her off her feet.

"Nope." Again, not exactly a lie, though definitely a stretch of the truth. The team members didn't use the ranks they'd attained before joining Task Force Zeta. The theory was that except for the commanding officer everyone on the team was to be considered equal.

"Oh." She pursed her lips and frowned deeper. "Hey, do you know any of those Navy SEALs? I'd love to meet one of them."

Matt thought of BB, the team's resident SEAL, and shook his head. "Nope. Sorry."

Again, not quite a lie. BB was on Zeta now, not on a SEAL team. And he had a wife and a new baby—not that Matt would have fixed his friend up with Wicked Wanda anyway, if that's what she'd been hinting at.

"Oh." She took a gulp of her drink, emptying the glass. "Well, it was nice meeting you, Matt, but I really should be going."

"Okay." Matt forced himself to hide his relief as he stood and extended a hand to her. "It was nice to meet you too."

Wanda stood so fast she nearly knocked her chair over. She shook his hand. "Thanks for the drink. I'll email you. Maybe we can get together again."

So he could buy her more drinks and then have her run off? Nope. Not gonna happen. Time for damage control.

"Sure. Do that." He put on a fake frown and slapped at his front and back jeans pockets, as if looking for his wallet. "Jeez, I hope I brought enough money with me. How much do you think the drinks cost?"

Her eyes opened wide. "Uh, I don't know. I'll ask the waiter to bring over the bill on my way out. Bye."

That had sent her running fast enough. Torn between guilt at his own dishonesty and relief over dodging a bullet, Matt crossed WickedWoman off his list of potential girlfriends.

He could only hope tomorrow's date with BabyGirl would be better.

With a sigh, Matt dug in his pocket for his wallet and pulled out his platinum card. Glancing in the direction of the bar, he spotted the waitress and signaled her for the check.

As he sat and waited for them to run his card, Matt punched in a text to Bull.

Date number one a dud.

Bull's response came back immediately.

Second time's the charm.

Matt could only hope Bull was right.

When had dating become such work? And not fun work either.

Usually, Matt was all over any sort of computer-related stuff. Research. Digging for details. It all made his adrenaline pump. Give him a code to crack or a secure database to hack and he was all over it. But this searching online for a good woman sucked.

A small pop heralded an instant message as it appeared on the screen of his cell.

Sam_I_am: *How's the big date?*

Matt snorted as he read it and typed in a response.

Computer_God: *It sucked!*

Sam_I_am: *It's done already?*

Computer_God: *Yes. Thank God.*

Sam_I_am: *Aw. Sorry.*

Knowing Sam well, Matt knew he was being sarcastic. Whatever. Matt was too miserable to care.

Maybe if Matt's teammates weren't pairing off like Noah's Ark had just pulled into port, he wouldn't feel like this. And perhaps if Matt hadn't been manning the communications console where he'd been forced to listen to, and in some cases watch on the surveillance camera not one but three of his teammates hook up with women, he wouldn't be so frustrated with his single status.

Jeez, three out of the six-man team. That had to be a record.

Or maybe not. Did all guys in charge of surveillance deal with this kind of shit? There was one person Matt knew he could ask.

Computer_God: *Hey. Question. Your guys ever hook up while on ops?*

Sam_I_am: *With each other???*

Computer_God: *No! With women.*

Sam_I_am: *Uh, no. What kind of ops you got going over there at Zeta?*

Matt sighed. That figured. He was the only one who had to listen to his teammates get laid, while all he'd laid his hands on lately was a computer console.

Sam_I_am: *Gotta go. Team moving in on a tango—not a woman. LOL! Later.*

Computer_God: *Later.*

At least somebody was having an exciting weekend.

The waitress returned with his card and receipt. Matt stood and pocketed both. Time to head home.

Maybe there was a good game on TV. He could sit and forget his dating woes.

CHAPTER THREE

Unlike Friday's date, Saturday's at least looked like her profile picture. Matt noticed that the moment BabyGirl arrived to join him, coincidentally at the same table where he'd sat with Wicked Wanda last night.

He hoped that wasn't a bad omen.

The young brunette extended her hand. "Hi. I'm Lisa. You must be Matt."

"I am. Nice to meet you, Lisa." He didn't let himself get too excited just because, unlike Wanda, Lisa had posted a photo taken during this decade.

He'd have to get to know her before he'd let himself start to envision anything past drinks tonight. One reason he remained wary was that Lisa had all the earmarks of being extremely high-maintenance.

Designer handbag, diamond watch, perfect highlighted and cut hair, manicured nails, clothes that probably cost what he made in a week.

Matt had grown up around girls like her. Spoiled princesses thanks to their father's money. He could spot a daddy's girl a mile away.

He pushed aside those thoughts. He shouldn't judge a book by its cover. He had to stay open minded or it was a certainty he'd also stay lonely.

Maybe she just liked to take good care of her appearance. He couldn't fault a girl for that.

Putting his first impressions firmly aside, Matt remained standing until she sat.

As he took his own seat, a waiter stopped at their table. "Do you need dinner menus or just drinks?"

"Oh, definitely menus," Lisa answered. "And a cosmopolitan to start, please."

All right. It seemed as if they were having dinner. And what was with the cosmopolitans? Weren't there any other drinks in the world? What was it with this drink and women?

Maybe it was because it was pink. Who knew?

"A beer for me, please." Matt ordered and then directed his attention back to Lisa. "I'm glad you could meet me tonight."

"Me too. Ever since I saw your profile, I've been dying to get to know you better." She leaned forward, looking like she meant what she said. "So, Matt. What do you do?"

Since it seemed all dates began with the same question, he decided to change things up a bit with a different answer than last time. "I work with computers."

"Really?" Her eyes opened wider. "I find that field fascinating."

"Eh, it's a living." Matt shrugged.

It seemed she was honestly interested in his work. That was good, or would be if his real career didn't take him around the world on next to no notice and wasn't so secret he'd never be able to tell her anything about it.

How the hell did the other guys do it?

Having a serious relationship in his line of work was going to be a challenge, to say the least.

Why was he trying to date again?

Oh, yeah. He remembered. Lack of sex and sheer boredom. Those were two powerful motivators.

The waiter returned with the menus and the drinks. Matt swallowed a mouthful of beer before he opened the menu on the table in front of him.

Hoping to deflect any further questions about his covert career, he thought he'd change the subject to something safe, such as food. "I've eaten here before and the fajitas are good. So's the burger. It comes with homemade sweet-potato fries that are good enough to make your mouth water."

Lisa opened her own menu and read, nodding as he talked.

The waiter returned. "Are you ready to order or do you need a few minutes?"

"I think I'm ready." Lisa looked up at their server. "I'll start with the Ahi Tuna appetizer and then the twin lobsters for an entrée."

Ahi and lobster—Apparently Lisa liked the stuff on the expensive side of the menu.

"Sir?"

Matt realized they were both waiting on his order. "Uh, chicken fajitas for me, please."

"Any appetizer?"

"Ah, yeah. Just a house salad. Italian dressing. Thanks."

The server nodded and left them alone again.

"Salad? I figured you for a chicken-wing kind of man." Lisa raised one perfectly shaped brow.

"I like to watch my figure." Matt grinned.

The truth was, he was too lazy to shop for groceries very often and the likelihood of there being anything organic besides mold in his fridge was pretty slim.

He ordered his healthy meals out and stuck to the two basic bachelor food groups at home—frozen food and beer. Those he could stock up on once a month without any fear they'd spoil before he got to eat them.

"I'm doing the low-carb thing." Lisa informed him of that while taking a nice big sip of her cocktail.

Matt didn't tell her how many empty calories or carbohydrates the alcohol and other assorted ingredients in her drink had.

Instead, he nodded. "Hence the lobster and tuna."

"Exactly." She smiled.

Matt couldn't shake how much Lisa reminded him of all

the girls who spent summers on Long Island—the summer paradise of New York.

Those girls had never even given him the time of day when he'd been younger. He was a surfer in a second-hand car who'd drive the hour from his parents' house every chance he got to catch the waves at Ditch Plains.

He'd sleep in his car or camp at Hither Hills, because back then he couldn't afford the overpriced rooms the tourists filled from Memorial Day through Labor Day. Not that there'd be any vacancies during the season anyway.

Maybe he was just oversensitive after last night's date, when Wanda had been more interested in his pay grade than his personality. He'd give Lisa the benefit of the doubt, even if she did order the most expensive things on the menu.

"Actually, my best friend just lost a ton of weight on that diet that Kate Middleton was on for her wedding. It's pretty interesting. You eat nothing at all except for lean meat for days—" As Lisa went on and on and on, Matt took another sip of beer.

The date was easy. Matt didn't have to do a thing except sit and listen to Lisa talk about herself, or her friends, or the food she hardly ever ate. Except, of course, for the tuna, and the butter-soaked lobster she devoured tonight while downing another calorie-laden cocktail, followed by a decaf cappuccino with a side of French cognac.

Matt didn't know which would be the bigger number, the amount of carbohydrates Lisa consumed on her supposed carb-free diet, or the price of her meal.

After he signaled for the check, Lisa leaned forward.

"I would never normally do this, but you seem so nice." She reached across the table and put her hand over his. "Would you mind coming back to my apartment?"

Mind? Hell no. He'd gladly accept that invitation.

He was about to express that sentiment in a more politically correct way when Lisa continued, "My computer has been acting funny. I think I might have picked up a virus. I keep getting error messages and crashing. The place where I bought it quoted me two hundred dollars to fix it. Isn't that crazy? I'm sure you could do it with no problem."

She smiled as he worked to keep his expression blank. She wanted him to come over to her place so he could give her free tech support? Just to save herself two hundred dollars?

That was probably what this date was going to cost him. It only seemed fair she should have to pay that amount to repair her own damn computer.

Had she been interested in him at all? Or just what he could do for her? How would Lisa even know if she were interested in him as a person since she'd basically talked at him rather than *to* him the entire dinner?

Matt forced a smile as his brain spun for a solution.

"I'd love to, Lisa. Oh, wait. Hold on a second. My cell phone is vibrating in my pocket. Excuse me." He turned sideways in his chair and held the phone to his ear. He pretended to speak to someone who was telling him about a very bad computer emergency that only he could handle. "Hang tight, Bob. I'll get there as soon as I can."

Matt pretended to disconnect the call with the phantom Bob.

Her eyes opened wide. "That sounded serious."

"I'm afraid it is. I'm so sorry, but I'm going to have to take a rain check. I have to go right away."

"I understand." She nodded. "I'll email you."

"Great. Do that." Not that he was planning to open anything she emailed him from her computer with the probable virus. "I'll take care of the bill on my way out. And it was great meeting you."

"Thank you. You too," she called after him as he waylaid the waiter on the way over with their check.

He waited at the hostess desk for them to run his card and give him his receipt and then made his escape.

Dating in the new millennium. Not only did a guy have to worry about catching sexually transmitted diseases, now he had to worry about getting infected with a computer virus.

He made it home and walked into his dark living room

feeling lower than before his great dating quest had begun.

The familiar chime on the computer he'd left on heralded an instant message.

The glow of the screen guided him across the room without the lights on. One glance at the screen had Matt scowling.

Sam_I_am: *You around?*

Computer_God: *Just walked in the door.*

Sam_I_am: *Home late from date. Good sign.*

Computer_God: *No, it's not. Bad date.*

Sam_I_am: *Sorry. More dates for next week?*

Matt considered his answer for a moment and then typed, *No!*

For extra emphasis, he added a half dozen more exclamation points and then hit send.

CHAPTER FOUR

Monday morning at zero-eight-hundred, Matt strolled into the meeting room happy to be at work after the hellish weekend he'd had in the dating trenches.

He stopped at the coffeemaker, filled his mug and then threw himself into a chair with a sigh.

Across the table, Trey Williams raised a brow. "Tough weekend?"

Matt snorted. "You have no idea."

"You should have come by the bar. Jack and I were there pretty much every night hanging out with Carly and watching baseball."

It sounded good in theory, but as each one of his teammates hooked up and got serious girlfriends, Matt felt more and more like a fifth wheel. "Was Nicki up visiting Jack?"

The reluctance to spend more time with the happy couples must have shown on Matt's face. A frown creased Trey's brow. "Why? You don't like Nicki?"

Matt shook his head. "No, it's not that. I like her a lot. And she's from New York like me. Around here, that's pretty rare. The thing is, I feel funny being the only single guy."

Trey rolled his eyes. "That's stupid. It's a bar. It's full of single guys. And you get used to Jack and Nicki disappearing upstairs to his apartment for an hour here and there. They always come back. As much as Jack likes sex, I think he likes a good game and a nice cold beer even better."

Maybe Matt should start to watch more sports and drink more to make up for the appalling lack of female companionship in his own life. He was just considering that when Jimmy came out of the commander's office.

"Well, boys. The commander is off doing something for Central Command, so I'm in charge for the next few days."

"Is there going to be any action?" Trey asked the question Matt was wondering the answer to himself.

"Nope. I swear it's like we're being punished for that party getting blown up with Bull inside." Jimmy didn't stop to address the misery that appeared in Bull's expression at that mention and continued, "We've got another training exercise this week and not much else. On top of that, they're fixin' to take Matt away from us."

Matt nearly choked on the swallow of coffee he'd just taken. "What? Me? Where am I going?"

Jimmy laughed. "Don't worry. They're not keeping you. You're on loan."

On loan? Like a frigging library book? "Ah, on loan to whom?"

Knowing Central Command, Matt could only imagine, and no scenario his brain came up with made him very happy.

"We'll go over it privately after the meeting. Now, for our next round of fun, how y'all feel about helping train some green SpecOp recruits by whooping their asses in a recon simulation?"

That brought smiles to the faces of every man in the room, except for Matt. He still couldn't help but wonder what his assignment would be.

Loaned out. What the fuck?

Matt stewed through the team meeting, right up until Jimmy dismissed the rest of the team except for him.

"Matt. Come on into the office." Jimmy led the way. He sat in the commander's chair and indicated Matt should sit in the other chair. "I gotta say, Coleman. This acting commander gig is pretty enlightening."

Jimmy's smirk had Matt frowning. "I'm not sure what you mean."

What the hell was Jimmy talking about and what did it have to do with Matt's assignment?

"Let's see. For starters, you never said you were recruited directly out of college for the Army's Delta Force Technology Unit. More importantly, I had no idea you'd developed—wait, let me get this straight—" Jimmy read from a single piece of paper he'd taken out of a manila folder, "—the technology for a targeting and guidance program for the military's new missile defense system. And you sold it to Uncle Sam for millions when you were nineteen." Jimmy put down the paper and frowned. "You're a freaking millionaire?"

That was in his personnel file? Matt had hoped Central wouldn't be quite so thorough in their paperwork. "I did have a partner in that project. We split the money from the contract."

Jimmy seemed to ignore Matt's explanation as he continued, "I mean, I knew you were smart, but not that you're a frigging prodigy. Like an actual certified genius. Graduating high school at sixteen, college at nineteen." Jimmy glanced up. "Three whole years to graduate valedictorian from college. What took you so long?"

Matt shrugged at Jimmy's sarcasm. "Well, you know. The missile program took up a lot of time, and we developed and sold a few computer games along the way too."

"Sure, in your spare time. Why not? I can understand that. Why not throw together a few games too." Shaking his head, Jimmy laughed.

"I'd appreciate it if we could keep all this information between us."

Jimmy narrowed his eyes. "Of course, but mind if I ask why? What's up? What's wrong?"

"I don't want to be treated differently. It's hard enough I'm safely tucked away in a van while you guys take fire."

"Matt, none of us are totally safe ever, you included. The baddies could take out that van with one well-placed missile."

"Thanks, Jimmy. I feel loads better now." Matt laughed.

Jimmy ignored the interruption. "And you and your computer genius have given us advantages on every single mission. You've kept all of us alive more times than I can count."

Matt let out a sigh. He knew what Jimmy said was true. It was just hard remembering it sometimes. "Thanks."

Jimmy slid a different folder forward. "Now, back to business. You're going to Dubai."

That news brought Matt's head up. "Dubai?"

"Yup. It seems as if our ally's air base in Dubai is having issues with the guidance system you—ahem—didn't invent and didn't make millions from." Jimmy winked at him. "Central wants you to go over there and give them a crash course. It should be quite an adventure. As a thank you for your special effort, the royal family has invited you to stay at one of their compounds."

"Really?" Wow. Not only was he getting out of the van, he was doing it in style.

Jimmy tossed a folder across the desk. Matt glanced inside. It contained information about Al Minhad Air Base, operated by the United Arab Emirates Air Force, though the British Armed Forces had operations there, as did the Aussies.

"Yup. I suggest you brush up on local customs. You leave right after our training mission with the new boys."

Matt grinned. It was going to be a very good week.

In a good mood after today's developments, Matt didn't even have the urge to check the dating site when he got home.

The last time he'd logged in and found a message from BabyGirl had pretty much cured his desire to ever go there again. The virus threat alone would have made him hit delete on Lisa's message, but the subject line that read Need Computer Help! had clinched it.

He'd deleted it unopened. Just because he had money

didn't mean he enjoyed spending it on a bad date whom only wanted him for his tech skills.

Research on Dubai kept Matt occupied for a solid hour after he got home. The royal family had their own website. Go figure.

He was just reading about Sheikh Mohammed's Internet City when a message from Sam popped up.

Sam_I_am: *Hey, not much time. Wanted you to know I'm going deep under. Can't talk for a while.*

Shit. The last time a member of Zeta went deep undercover, they had to rescue him. They'd been a little late and Jimmy had come back by way of the military hospital in Germany. And now Sam was going.

Computer_God: *Watch your ass. Okay?*

Sam_I_am: *Will do, at least until I find someone else to watch it for me. Later.*

Computer_God: *Later.*

At least this time, Matt didn't have to be envious of Sam's mission because he had a kick ass one of his own.

Sam would be turning a little green with envy at Matt's assignment if he knew about it. Being a guest in a royal compound while training some foreign techy how to use a computer program he'd invented—it was like winning the SpecOp lottery. Piece of cake.

Meanwhile, Sam was going deep undercover, headed into God only knew what kind of trouble. Matt sat back in his chair and blew out a long, slow breath, hoping whatever Sam's assignment turned out to be, it didn't cost Matt his friend.

CHAPTER FIVE

Sam Foster had just closed the IM window with Zeta team's comm guy, Matt Coleman, when Task Force Omega's commander stepped up to the desk.

Commander Anderson smiled. "You ready, Foster?"

"Yes, sir." She'd been preparing for this kind of an assignment her entire career in Special Operations.

Communications personnel on the various special task forces set in place after the terror attacks of September eleventh rarely got to see much hands-on action, let alone go deep undercover. But for once, rather than being tied to a computer, Sam was going in. Alone.

To say infiltrating without any team backup was frightening would be the understatement of the century, even though the assignment was in a supposed friendly zone.

In the Gulf, friendly could become very unfriendly in the blink of an eye—especially for a woman. But Sam had been working as a female in a male-dominated world for a while now. She was ready.

Her commander cocked his head toward the door of his office. "Come on inside for a sec."

Sam nodded.

For the first time in the six months she'd been Omega's comm officer, Commander Anderson seemed to be treating her with kid gloves—treating her like a woman rather than a capable member of his team.

She didn't like it one bit. She'd fought to be equal her entire career in the service. What burned her ass and confused the entire equal-rights issue was that the reason she was going to Dubai undercover was because they needed a tech-savvy female, specifically, for the assignment and she fit the bill.

He led the way to his office and sat behind the desk. "Take a seat."

She sat in the chair opposite her commander as he stared at her without speaking. "Sir?" Nothing like silence from a superior officer to make a person nervous. "Samantha..."

Now he was calling her by her full first name. Not good. "Yes, commander?"

He shook his head. "If you weren't a woman I'd be slapping you on the back and sending you off without thinking twice about it."

"I know, sir." She kept her expression blank in the face of what she knew was sexist but true.

"But the fact is, you are a woman, and I'm sending you deep undercover into a damn harem in the middle of Dubai with no backup and without the knowledge of our allied forces in the region."

That about covered it. She swallowed a nervous impulse to laugh. Now that he put it that way, it did sound pretty crazy and damn scary.

Commander Anderson ran both hands over his face. "Maybe we need to bring someone over there into the loop, just to be safe—"

"No." Sam shook her head. "The reason I'm going in is because we don't know who we can trust. The transmissions I intercepted originated from somewhere within that compound. We don't know who sent them. It could be a guard or a gardener . . . but for all we know, it could be the sheikh himself."

Dubai was their ally. Yet someone from within one of the

residences used regularly by the royal family had been contacting known terrorists. Central Command needed to find out whom.

He drew in a deep breath. "I know, and if I was sending one of the others, I wouldn't think twice about it."

"Because they're men and I'm a woman." This song was starting to get pretty old.

The commander could talk all he wanted, beat himself up until she left and got back again, but it wouldn't change the facts. Sam had girl parts, not a penis, and that was why they needed her for this assignment.

"I feel like I'm pimping you out, Foster." The commander looked as if he were in physical pain saying it. "It's a harem. There's a chance you might . . . the situation may arise . . ." He obviously found the thought so horrendous he couldn't finish the sentence.

She wasn't going into the harems of old. The ones with the silk veils and dancing girls and public baths.

All of their sources and her research indicated this modern-day version was less harem and more Playboy Mansion. Young pretty women, often models or actresses, gathered by the royal family more as window dressing for their important guests.

"I'm not a virgin, sir."

He laughed. "Thanks, I hadn't even considered that possibility."

Sam wasn't sure if she should feel insulted or flattered by his reaction to her declaration on the state of her virginity, or lack thereof.

She decided to let it go. "What I'm saying, sir, is that I'll do what I have to do, whatever that is, to get the job done. But I'm smart and I'm well-trained, and I've even been told by a few people I'm clever. I'll get the information we need and get out, hopefully with the virtue you're concerned about intact."

Okay, so maybe she was enjoying the blush on the commander's face at her virtue comment.

A woman couldn't spend as many hours as she did in such close quarters with all these alpha males without getting a thick skin.

But in spite of being surrounded by prime beef all day every day, Sam never partook of any of her Omega teammates, nor would she. Actually, she'd found herself fantasizing about a guy she'd never even met.

Strange but true, her buddy Computer_God had provided her with plenty of fantasies on the nights she'd whipped out her trusty vibrator. Her internet skills had even yielded a photo of him for her to use for her mental imagery.

"Have you . . . ah, did you visit medical?"

Sam forced her mind back to her red-faced commander. "Yes, sir."

"And did you get the . . . um . . . required implant?" He rushed through the end of the sentence.

She was glad he'd broken eye contact, because she felt herself start to blush too. Commander Anderson wasn't that much older than herself, not old enough to be her father or anything. But he was her superior, which made it feel kind of like having a conversation about birth control with her father. That made this entire discussion far different than hearing the guys on the team tell dirty jokes or comment on the size of the waitress's breasts at the local hangout.

Sam composed herself and answered. "Yes, sir. I did."

She'd lost track of how many implants she'd had put inside her since joining the covert team—communications, tracking—but this was the first time she'd been ordered to get one designed for birth control. Another thing that made her unequal to her male teammates. Although she supposed medical would have handed them a box of condoms instead before they were sent into a harem.

Sam raised her gaze and found her commander watching her again. "It's going to be fine. Trust me."

"I do trust you, Foster." He laughed, though it somehow sounded sad. "It's the rest of the world I don't trust."

Wasn't that the truth . . .

CHAPTER SIX

The compound sometimes used by His Highness Sheikh Mohammed and his numerous family members and guests was impressive, to say the least.

Matt had been driven into the complex past the horse-training facility. Arabs took the breeding and racing of their horses as seriously, if not more so, than Americans. Matt took a moment to digest the surreal reality that not too long ago he'd been at Jack and Jimmy Gordon's family horse farm in Pigeon Hollow and now he was here.

Sometimes his life was just plain strange. Maybe he'd get a tour of the barns and then he could email and tell the Gordons all about it.

The servant led Matt through what should be called a palace but was only one of many residences used by the royal family. The polite but quiet local man, who spoke more perfect English than half the guys on Zeta, escorted Matt down marble hallways.

The first thing that struck Matt as he passed various security points was that the compound was well outfitted with technology. Unlike some of the ops he'd worked on, there'd be no crawling on roof tops to set up temporary satellite communications. No running wires out of windows.

Matt wouldn't even have to work out of the usual

cramped van. Not on this trip. Not when you were the guest of a sheikh.

They ended the tour at the collection of rooms he'd be staying in during this assignment.

Matt walked past the king-sized bed in the bedroom and out onto the private balcony to check out the view. That was *after* he'd taken particular note of the computer with the double flat-screen monitors in the living area.

His balcony overlooked a secluded garden decorated with fountains and exotic-looking flowers.

This was one hell of a setup and Matt intended to enjoy every second of it. His only regret as he glanced back at the silk-draped bed was that he had no one here with him to share it.

He stepped from the scorching heat on the terrace and back into the cooler air of the bedroom.

There was an English version of the biography of Sheikh Mohammed on the bedside table—for his reading pleasure he supposed.

He walked past that and into the living area. Not that he wasn't interested in the life story of Dubai's ruler, but he'd far rather get his hands on the computer.

How sick would a video game look on that huge screen? Too bad he couldn't instant message Sam and brag about it.

He had arrived here mid-morning, but he needn't have worried about not having anything to do for the rest of the day because there was an entire itinerary planned for him.

After his tour of the compound and the time he was given to settle into his room, he was driven to the air base.

There, he spent the afternoon reviewing the guidance system with the personnel. That's when he figured out the system wasn't working even for him.

It must have been installed wrong. He started the reinstallation, but they were going to run all night.

Matt left the tech guys with instructions to call him if anything funky happened and a promise to be back first thing in the morning.

Finally, he arrived back at his room exhausted from both the travel and a full day.

He'd just walked in the door when a food tray arrived, served by none other than a girl dressed like that Disney princess from Aladdin—bare belly, flowing pants, sheer scarves covering her face, the whole shebang.

If this was what waitresses looked like here in Dubai, it blew away those at Hooters back in the States. His team would never believe it. He had to fight the urge to snap a picture with his cell phone for the guys back home.

She hovered in the doorway, holding the tray and apparently waiting for instruction.

"Um, thanks. You can just put it over there."

She did as asked but didn't leave after setting down the tray. Nor did she make a move to go after laying out the utensils, napkin and the plate of food on the table in front of a window in the room.

Matt said thank you one more time, first in English and then in her native language, wondering if maybe she didn't understand him. He wasn't the language expert like Trey. Matt knew enough Arabic to get by if he had to, but not much more.

The woman inclined her head in a bow. "I am here to serve you."

She'd surprised him with her careful English. He glanced at the table she'd laid out so nicely for him. "Yes, and you did it very well. Thank you."

Still she didn't leave. Maybe she was trained like the proper British butlers in movies and would stand there in case he needed more water or fresh ground pepper or something.

Fine. She could stand and watch him eat if that was her job. He didn't want her to get in trouble.

"So, nice weather today." Feeling more than a bit self-conscious, he attempted some small talk.

Her response was a nod.

"It's very beautiful here. It must be a nice place to work."

Even if she did have to dress like that.

Again, she nodded but didn't speak.

Out of things to say, Matt ate the rest of his meal in silence.

When he had finished the last of the food, she cleared the table and loaded everything back onto the tray. With one final tip of her head, she headed for the door.

"Thanks, again," Matt called at her back and then sighed with relief at being alone again.

With a nice full belly, he'd be very happy to get to bed. Maybe after a little computer time.

He stood, excited about his plan for the remainder of the evening, when he realized she'd handed the tray to someone in the hall and had come back in. She peered at him with big brown eyes that continued to dart down to stare at the floor.

Now what?

"The meal was excellent. Thank you. Please give my compliments to the chef. But I'm so full I don't think I'll want anything more to eat tonight. Thank you."

"I am here to serve you." She inclined her head again and didn't move.

Okay. He got that, but dinner was over. Was she going to hang around until his breakfast tray arrived?

She finally raised her gaze to meet his. It was the boldest move she'd made all night.

"I'm to serve you . . . in there." She pointed toward the bedroom door.

Matt's heart skipped a beat. Holy shit. Was she a legitimate harem girl? Did they still exist?

Apparently they did, because here she was, dressed like that, pointing toward the room with the giant bed. He swallowed and tried not to notice the large expanse of her exposed skin and the tempting curves that were so not covered by all that see-through fabric.

Holy moly. Were those her nipples showing through?

Wasn't this ironic? Matt had spent all last weekend on dates from hell, hoping to get laid, and here he was on assignment with a harem girl and he wasn't sure what to do with her.

Crap. He'd probably risk insulting his host if he rejected this more than generous though odd as hell gift.

The team trained that when immersed in a foreign culture you went along with the local customs. So if they considered monkey brains a delicacy and fed that to him for dinner, he would have to eat monkey brains and tell them how good they tasted.

But did it also mean that if he was handed a harem girl to service him, he was supposed to let her?

Why the hell was he having trouble convincing himself to take her up on her offer?

This was what he'd wished for, kind of—to hook up with a hot chick on assignment like his teammates kept doing.

But the other guys just happened to meet the girl of their dreams while on a mission. This seemed more like she was a hooker and Matt was the john, which made the sheikh the pimp in this scenario. Not good.

Matt looked her over again. Was she forced into this or did she do it willingly?

Life for a woman in Saudi Arabia could be tough. Circumstances could make giving her body to strange men in exchange for plenty of food and a safe place to live the only option for this girl.

He couldn't take advantage of her or her situation.

Besides, he enjoyed the thrill of the chase. He liked going out on a date and trying to hook up. Being handed a girl as a gift didn't seem right.

Damn. How could he get out of this without single-handedly destroying international relations? "Um. I wouldn't mind a back and maybe a foot massage. Could you do that? Give me a massage?"

That request seemed safe enough.

She nodded, reached out and offered him her hand.

He took it and let her lead him to the bedroom, where Matt began to wonder if she'd understood him. It was very likely *massage* had different connotations here.

When she unbuttoned his shirt and reached for his pants, he got even more nervous. On instinct, he reached down and stilled her hands at his fly.

"Pants get in the way of the massage," she said.

"But just a massage, right?" he asked.

She nodded. "I understand. Massage."

Matt hesitated for a moment and then sat on the edge of the bed to pull off his shoes and socks. He stood again and dropped his pants, diving face down onto the bed in his briefs before she got the idea his underwear would interfere with the massage too.

He heard her move and turned his head to see her reach into the drawer of the bedside table and pull out a bottle of oil. Brow raised, he wondered what else was in there. He'd have to investigate that when she left.

Expertly warming the oil in her hands before applying it to his back, she set to work on his travel-weary muscles.

She must have been trained in massage, as well as the other things he hesitated to imagine. It wasn't too bad.

In fact, he could get used to this kind of treatment after a hard day of hunching over a computer keyboard. She worked his shoulders, hard and deep. The woman had magic hands.

Moving down, she treated every knot until the tension eased. She moved down farther and kneaded his lower back.

A moan escaped him when she hit on one area that had been bothering him since he'd strained it during a team workout last week. It made him feel so good, so relaxed, Matt considered asking if she could come back again tomorrow for a repeat.

She slipped her hands beneath the waistband of his underwear and his breath caught in his throat. She began to work his glutes.

Not shy, she dug right in while Matt held his breath.

It was just another muscle. Right? He tried to convince himself of that.

She worked her way lower, her well-oiled thumbs

spreading his cheeks. He felt the cool air of the room hitting a private spot that he didn't want exposed to anyone. Certainly not a stranger during a massage.

When her fingertip pressed against his tight hole, Matt flipped over. "That's enough. Thanks."

"I do the front now." She poured more oil into her hand and Matt realized his mistake. He'd covered his rear, but he'd exposed his front.

Before she could touch anything else, such as the burgeoning erection he prayed would stay down, he said, "No. That's really—"

Ignoring his protest, she reached and grabbed his arm, beginning to work on the biceps.

Arms were good. Nice and safe. He could handle that.

Eyes closed, he tried to relax as she glided over his chest, soothing away the tension there.

Then the downward descent began again, and she slipped one hand beneath the elastic of his briefs. His eyes flew open about the same time his cock reacted to her touch.

Her well-oiled fingers grasped him as he watched, horrified when he realized he was doing nothing to stop her.

She slid her hands up and down his length until he was totally aroused and appalled.

Matt drew in a shaky breath. "What are you doing?"

She looked at him but her fingers never stopped. "Massage."

Oh, boy.

As his mind reeled, he dropped his head back on the pillow.

Breathing heavy, he argued with himself. Maybe this was just part of a normal Dubai massage.

In her eyes, there could be nothing sexual about this. It was just a massage.

Yeah, right. Just a massage during which she took her other hand and began to tug on his balls while she fisted his shaft.

She'd do anything and everything he asked sexually—

instinctively he knew. It was her job, and it was because of that he'd vowed to not take advantage of her.

He could let her finish. It wouldn't take very long. In spite of his thinking he didn't want this, the feel of someone else's hands on his dick besides his own was too much for him to resist. And if he sent her away now, he could risk insulting the host who'd sent her, who most likely was a member of the royal family.

She'd already had her hands all over him. Would stopping her before he came make any difference?

Yes. It would to him.

Matt sat up and grabbed her wrist. "Thank you. I'm good. You can go now."

He watched her brow furrow. "I displease you. My apologies."

"No, you don't displease me. You please me very much." As evidenced by the protrusion tenting his briefs. "But I don't usually have women service me like you were doing. Do you understand?"

An expression of relief showed clearly on her face. She nodded. "Yes, I understand. I will leave you."

"Thank you. And, uh, thanks for the massage." He let out a slow breath as she backed out of the room, her eyes downcast.

The door closed and Matt flung himself backward onto the mattress, considering if he was noble or a fool.

Either way, he had no intention of telling a soul about this. Not that they'd believe him anyway. A freaking harem girl. Jeez.

Matt forced himself to sit up. He still had a situation to deal with. Grabbing the bottle of oil she'd left on the nightstand, he slid off the high bed.

It was lonely on the moral high ground. Matt realized that as he, his bottle of oil and his hard-on headed for the bathroom.

He worked his length with one oiled hand and allowed himself the leeway of envisioning her incredible body beneath the barely there outfit. As torn as he was about the whole incident, his mind still turned to the feel of her hands on him.

That did it. He was done for. Matt came hard and fast into his own golden toilet. It was one hell of a fucked-up experience all around.

He'd just finished his own personal massage when there was a knock on the bathroom door. The sound made him jump. He'd have to remember that privacy here at the compound was just an illusion. He slipped on a robe and opened the door.

Standing before him, head down, was a young, dark-haired boy. He looked to be about in his late teens.

"Hi. Can I help you?"

The boy bowed his head. "Jasmine sent me."

Who the hell was Jasmine?

"Um. Okay. What did she send you to do?"

The dinner dishes had been taken away already. Maybe this kid was supposed to turn down the bed and leave a chocolate on the pillow.

"She said you would prefer me to service you, rather than her."

Matt felt the blood drain from his face as realization hit.

This place gave room service a whole new meaning. Shit. He should have just let Jasmine finish the job.

Now what? He definitely wasn't letting this kid . . . he couldn't even finish the thought in his own head.

Damn it. They should have covered this kind of cultural shit better in training. He'd rather eat monkey brains than have to dance around in this sexual mine field the whole time he was here.

His head still down, the boy waited for Matt's response.

"How old are you?" Matt asked.

"Eighteen."

At least he wasn't a child. He only looked like one. Another thought flitted across Matt's brain that nearly made him ill. He hoped to God that if this boy was being sent to service men, that he at least preferred men.

To be prostituted was bad enough, but to be forced to do something against his very nature, that was inhuman.

Matt had to find out. If this place was a center for some sort of sex-slave trade, he could do something about it.

It would be a mess—his exposing the leader of Dubai as running a sex ring wouldn't disturb international relations too much, yeah right—but he'd do it.

"Sit down." Matt indicated a chair across the room.

The boy turned, walked to the chair, sat and waited.

Another horrible notion crossed Matt's mind. What if the boy assumed he'd been asked to sit so his mouth would be crotch level with a standing man?

As fast as he could, Matt sat himself in a chair far across the room.

The boy lifted his gaze and an expression of confusion settled on his face.

"You wish to ask me something." It was more statement than question. Luckily, the boy spoke first. Matt was having trouble finding words.

"Do they . . . force you to do this? Make you come to me, to others, against your will?"

He smiled at Matt. "You think I am being forced?"

"Yes." Matt nodded. "You're not?"

"No, not at all. It is seen as a great honor to service a guest of the royal family. When Jasmine told me of her dilemma, I offered to come." He lowered his head. "If I don't please you, I can send one of the others."

Shit. There were more of them?

Matt tried not to think about how boys and girls from all over the complex were lining up somewhere to service him. And how every one he turned away would see it as a rejection, worthy of shame.

This was too much responsibility. Maybe the British tech guy he'd worked with today had a room for him to stay in. Hell, he'd sleep with the computers if he had to.

He'd consider that tomorrow. Tonight, there was an ever-worsening situation to repair.

"What's your name?" Matt asked.

"Rashid."

"Rashid, can I tell you a secret, just between us men?"

The boy nodded.

"I don't um, lie with men. I prefer women." Matt's cheeks were probably about as red as the covering on his bed thanks to this crazy conversation.

Rashid's eyes opened wide. "I understand now. You did not like Jasmine but did not want to hurt her by saying so. You are a very kind man."

Close enough. Matt nodded. "You won't tell Jasmine or her, uh, boss, will you? I don't want to get her into trouble."

"No, sir. I won't tell. But people will notice if I leave here too soon. The guard outside . . ."

There was a guard outside? That was freaking news and raised the question of whether the guard was to keep him in or others out.

He pushed that out of his mind to consider later. Right now, Matt had to kill some time with Rashid so no more sexual gifts would be delivered tonight.

"Hey, Rashid, do you ever get to play computer games?" By the huge saucer-eyed look he got, Matt determined the answer was no. "I could show you how to play one, if you'd like."

Vigorous nodding followed, so Matt made his way across the room to the computer.

As he booted it up, he couldn't help but think he would never, ever complain about being stuck in the van again. If this kind of shit was what being in the thick of the action entailed, the other guys could have it.

CHAPTER SEVEN

Sam had intended to slip around the palace as much as she could.

The moment she arrived she knew her plan wouldn't work. It would be impossible to move about unnoticed. The sheer amount of electronic surveillance as well as guards guaranteed that.

"This is where you'll live." Sam's guide, a man dressed in servants' garb, stopped outside a closed door. He set down her bag, nodded and left.

All righty.

Sam bent to retrieve her single piece of luggage from the floor and opened the door. It was like stepping back in time, right down to the dozen or so girls in harem outfits staring as she stood in the doorway.

"Come in. Quickly. Shut the door."

"Okay." Sam took a step in and closed the door.

"Men can't see the girls unless the sheikh says they may."

"Oh. Sorry." Sam extended her hand. "I'm Sabrina."

"Yes, of course. I was told to expect a new girl. You may call me Ana. You'll need something to wear." The older woman ignored the bag in Sam's hand.

"I packed a variety of clothes. Dressy. Casual."

"No. In the past, yes, western clothing would have been fine, but not now. The sheikh has a very important guest staying here. Royalty who prefers the old ways, so we comply."

This was not good news, because the old way was apparently nearly naked.

Physically, Sam was in good shape. She worked out enough so she should be. Showing off a toned body in a bathing suit was one thing, but showing off her nipples for royal guests in a palace was quite another.

Ana reached behind an ornate screen and came out with a costume to match what the other girls wore. "Here. This should work with your coloring. You'd be more popular with the men if you had more curves. You have to eat. For now, they may be intrigued enough with your blonde hair and blue eyes to overlook you're built like a boy. Then again, there are those who prefer the boys who may like you, as well."

When Sam didn't move to change, Ana frowned. "Get dressed. What are you waiting for? He expects you now."

"Who expects me?"

"Jefri, Prince of Brunei."

As she slipped behind the screen, Sam's mind spun, remembering something she'd read years ago about Brunei and its royal family.

It was rumored that they partied like Hugh Hefner, surrounded by beautiful women from all over the world. To the best of Sam's recollection, the current sultan's brother, Prince Jefri, had been accused of embezzling billions of dollars, besides other allegations of the more sexual nature. Disgraced, Jefri had fled his country.

And now this prince from Brunei was a guest of the royal family of Dubai and wanted her to come to him . . . dressed like this.

Holy shit, this was not what Sam had expected. It was enough to make her head spin.

There was no mirror, so how was she supposed to know how she looked in this outfit? Perhaps it was better that she didn't know.

She stepped out from behind the screen to find Ana

nodding. "Good. Let's go."

Maybe this prince just liked to welcome all the new girls. Sam tried to convince herself of that during the walk through some private hallways leading to another closed door.

When Ana knocked, a guard opened it to them.

Two things told Sam she might be in trouble here, in addition to the heavily armed guard. First, the sunken bathing tub filled with naked women. And second, the equally nude man who must be the prince himself.

"Eyes down," Ana hissed the order. "And remember, the sheikh wants his guests kept happy, no matter what."

"Yes, ma'am."

Ana wasn't much of an ally, but once she had gone, Sam realized how alone she was. She should have let the commander contact someone here when he'd brought it up.

"Come here. Let me see you." Prince Jefri's intense stare took her in from head to toe, pausing at plenty of places in between during his perusal.

Eyes down, she took one step forward.

"You're too thin," he said.

So she'd been told. "My apologies."

"Come closer."

Swallowing hard, she took another step.

Her gaze caught on the expression of the three women in the giant tub. Two looked curious, while pure hatred radiated off one. Perfect. Just what Sam needed. Jealousy.

Apparently, the prince's main squeeze viewed her as competition and hated her on sight. Little did this woman know, Sam would be more than happy to let her have the prince all to herself.

He hoisted himself out of the water, naked as the day he was born and fully aroused. He came to her and grasped her chin, raising it. "Blue eyes. Real? Or are they contact lenses?"

"Real." For the first time in her life, Sam wished they weren't.

Nodding, he released her chin. He circled to stand behind her. She didn't like not being able to see him.

He trailed a finger from a spot between her shoulder blades, down to the small of her back. He continued down the crack between her ass cheeks, the laughably sheer fabric of her harem pants the only barrier between her and his unwelcome touch.

The sudden feel of Jefri's hand on her belly as he reached around her had Sam sucking in a sharp breath. He slid his hand up and cupped her breast. "The tits are obviously real."

His hands-on inspection didn't end there. After giving her breast a painful squeeze he slipped his hand down and beneath the pants riding low on her hips.

He continued until he'd slid it inside her, breaching her with one thick finger. "Nice. Tight. Good."

She held herself completely still, barely breathing as he violated her with that single probing digit.

The urge was strong to fight. One move and she could break his nose . . . which would no doubt lead to the guard breaking her in many places.

Pressing against her back, he was so close she smelled the wine on his breath.

As the water from his skin soaked through her thin clothing and his erection pressed against her ass, Jefri said against her ear, "Eat more."

He slid the finger out of her and took a step back.

If he'd felt the thundering of her heart as the adrenaline pounded through her veins, he didn't say so.

This was just a temporary reprieve. Sam knew that. If Jefri decided to bend her over and take her here and now, she'd do it. She'd have to.

Shamed though Jefri had been in his own country, he was here as a guest of the royal family of Dubai. She couldn't insult him or deny him what he wanted. They'd all been trained to withstand torture. She'd withstand this too.

To object to whatever he asked of her could get Sam thrown out, or worse, expose her cover and get her killed. She was there for a reason—and if ever there was a man with motive to sell secrets, it was this one.

"She's pretty, no?" Jefri asked the girls in the tub.

"Not particularly," the one giving her the hate-filled stares answered.

Jefri chuckled while patting Sam's ass.

"I will look forward to getting to know you better." He left Sam, went back to the tub and sat on the edge next to the woman shooting daggers from her eyes. He barely glanced at her when he said, "You may go."

Sam dipped her head in a nod. She was about to turn toward the door when the prince grasped the woman's head and pushed her mouth down over his thick erection. "Now, you bad girl. Show the others what happens to girls with sharp tongues."

The guard's hand on her elbow brought Sam's attention around. She was more than happy to let him lead her out.

During the walk back to Ana, Sam realized she needed to get what she'd come to do done and get the hell out of here. The sooner the better.

But how with guards and cameras everywhere?

If she'd learned anything being in the military, it was to adapt and overcome. She needed a new plan of action. If she couldn't roam the compound searching for their target, whoever was corresponding with known terrorist cells, she'd find another way.

Even if she had to listen to every bit of gossip about the residents and employees at the compound. Even if she had to let that vile man put his hands on her, she would for the mission.

The guard left her at the end of the private hallway, once again outside the door to the room that she hated to call the harem. The camera aimed at the door told her there was no way she could go wandering around even if she were alone.

Shaking, Sam knocked on the door and it was once again opened.

"What did he say?" Ana was there immediately, demanding a report.

"I should eat more."

One sharp brow cocked up. "Just as I said." Ana's lips formed a thin, hard line. "First the American guest turns away my best girl in favor of a slip of a boy who now talks of nothing but the computer games he played with him. And now, they send me a girl built like a boy."

"Wait. An American? Is here?"

"Yes. He arrived yesterday. He sent Jasmine away, so I gave him Rashid."

Her pulse pounded at the revelation.

Sam needed to discover the identity of this American man and his purpose for being here.

"Maybe I should be sent to the American man." She should be safe enough going to investigate if he liked boys. She could get a look at him, try to gather some intel and get out of there. No problem.

Ana narrowed her gaze. "What good would that do? I told you, he rejected Jasmine."

"Yes, but as you've said, he prefers boys and I'm built like a boy." Finally, Sam's thin, flat-chested figure was good for something in this harem.

Ana smiled. "Good. Bring him his dinner and remain as long as he wishes." She opened the door and a guard appeared. "Take her to the kitchen and then to the American in the Palm Suite."

CHAPTER EIGHT

Matt's second day on loan at least felt more productive than the first had. He was able to troubleshoot the guidance system and figure out why it still wasn't operating correctly even after the reinstall.

Once he'd figured out there was something in the program that wasn't compatible with another system they'd installed, he could work to correct the issue.

In Matt's defense, he had developed this for US government use, not to be able to work with this other technology the foreign military had deployed to their servers. But this program was his baby, so he worked his ass off to fix it and save face—his own as well as his government's.

It was evening by the time he got back to his room, tired, with his ass dragging.

After his fucked up day, he could only hope he wouldn't have more gifts from his absent host to contend with. He'd be very happy with nothing more than a hot shower and bed. Maybe dinner too, if it happened to show up at his door and didn't come with a sex slave attached.

The shower would come first. The muscles in his back and neck ached, and the short time he'd been out in the heat had drenched his shirt in sweat.

He bypassed the bathtub that sat on a raised platform and overlooked the gardens in favor of the separate shower stall. The tub would take forever to fill. It was so big he could entertain an entire harem in it.

That he'd allowed that thought to cross his mind *and* that the idea appealed to him proved the extent of his exhaustion. Or maybe just how sexually deprived he was.

Dammit. He was such a loser.

He'd been jealous of all the guys on his team as they'd hooked up and got girlfriends because they were all getting steady sex. And now, when he'd been handed the opportunity to have not only sex, but crazy harem-girl sex, what did he do? He kicked her out of his room and had gone out of his way to convince his host he was gay. All to assure they didn't send him any more women.

Maybe one day he'd stop getting in his own damn way and just enjoy his good fortune.

Matt stripped down as the water ran in a shower stall large enough to bathe an elephant. Frustrated, he ducked his head under the hot spray and let the water pound on the back of his neck.

Eyes closed, his mind began to drift to the night before. Not to Rashid learning how to play his first video game, but to before that, when Jasmine had him clasped in her warm, oil-covered hand . . . right before he'd told her to stop.

He was definitely the stupidest genius he knew.

The sound of the bathroom door opening had Matt tensing.

Who the hell would it be this time? Rashid with his dinner, maybe? Though that wouldn't require a visit to him in the shower. Both the video games the kid had enjoyed so much and the table where Matt ate were out in the other room.

Matt turned his head to peer through the thick steam. The stall was so large it didn't have a curtain or doors. The water simply couldn't reach far enough to splatter the rest of the massive bathroom.

Even with the swirling steam, he could make out his

visitor wasn't Rashid.

Nope, she was definitely a female and as she moved closer he got an even better look at her. All of her, because the sheer outfit revealed possibly more than Jasmine's had.

Meanwhile, Matt was well aware that he was completely exposed, his fantasy induced hard-on and all.

This woman was leaner than Jasmine. She had blonde hair and a piercing blue gaze that dropped to take all of him in. Those eyes crinkled in the corners when she smiled.

His breath caught in his throat as she came toward him, stripping what masqueraded as her clothing as she approached until she was nude and oh so tempting.

She stepped into the stall and pressed her very naked front to his back as he faced the spray. She wrapped her arms around him from behind.

Matt was tall, but so was she. The length of her body pressed against his. He braced against the wall with both hands as, much more forward than Jasmine had been, this woman pinched one of his nipples while her other hand strayed down his abdomen.

Somewhere in his muddled mind, he realized he was going to let this happen. He held on to his last shred of decency and said, "You don't have to do this."

"Shh. I want to." Her voice came soft and sultry from somewhere just behind his ear.

Strange that she had no hint of an accent. As strange as her fair hair compared to the darker coloring of Jasmine and Rashid.

When she wrapped her hand around him all questions fled from his mind.

She brushed her lips against the side of this throat before she latched her teeth onto his earlobe.

Matt let out a groan. "You need to stop."

Her hand on him paused just long enough for her to ask, "Don't you find me attractive?"

"I find you incredibly attractive. I think that's pretty obvious. But you still need to stop."

She tightened her grip around him. "Why?"

"Because it's not right. You're doing this because you've been told to." Inside him, the devil and the angel warred.

Matt wasn't quite sure which had won. He'd told her to stop, but he'd also let her hand remain, slowly stroking up and down his hard length.

"A man with morals." She slid the tip of one finger along the slit in the top of his cock and dragged in a ragged breath. "Matt Coleman, I think I like you even more than I did before."

He tensed. Something wasn't right here. "You know my name?"

She pressed her mouth against his ear. "Don't react. I'm not sure if the suite has eyes and ears."

Not only did her speech sound distinctly American, but she'd just told him in the SpecOp shorthand he used daily that his room might have audio and video surveillance in place.

Naked and unarmed with his back to a stranger who held his dick in her hands—he'd get what he deserved if he ended up dead for this act of extreme stupidity.

He should be able to overpower—

"Matt, relax. It's me. Sam," the woman hissed in his ear over the sound of the pounding water.

"I don't know any Sam." He angled his head toward her, calculating how best to go about taking her down. If only she'd stop stroking his cock.

He would have thought the fright of dying would have taken care of his hard-on. It didn't, nor would it. Not if she kept this up, whoever she was.

She ran her hands up into the hair that curled around his ears and pulled his head to one side, giving her access to his ear. "You frigging idiot. I'm Sam_I_am. You're Computer_God. Jeez. Make a girl feel forgettable much?"

"Sam?" That information nearly sent him to his knees on the marble floor. "You're female?"

His good buddy Sam? Not just female, but hot and naked,

not to mention pressed firmly against him with his dick in her hand.

"Uh, yes. Sam is for Samantha." She laughed against his ear. He shivered in spite of the hot water still pummeling him. "You didn't know?"

Oh, boy. This added a whole other level of complications to the situation. He pulled her hand away from his cock and turned. She rested her palms on his chest, running them up and down his wet skin.

"Nope. Definitely did not know." His erection was still alive and well, in spite of everything going on in his head. It stuck out straight as an arrow between them. There wasn't much Matt could do about the situation, except ignore it and hope it would go away while he gathered some answers. "What are you doing here?"

She leaned in closer to his ear. "Talk softer. I don't know how sensitive their equipment is. The water should cover it if we whisper. And I told you on instant messenger I was going deep. Remember?"

Her comment about going deep while her hardened nipples pressed against him sent his mind to bad, bad places.

He shouldn't be thinking about being buried deep inside his good buddy Sam, but he was. Especially when she slipped the tip of her tongue into his ear. He supposed it was all in case there were surveillance cameras, but his body didn't care.

Goose bumps rose on his skin from the contact.

He nuzzled her neck and asked, "How did you know I was here?"

"I came to investigate the American visitor. I carried in your dinner tray and saw your name and address on your luggage tag. I take it you're not undercover, so what the fuck are you doing here?"

It was a simple enough question, though he had trouble forming an answer while she slid her hands over his ass and pressed her body from tits to thigh against his.

Matt sucked in a breath and tried to think. "I'm working at Al Minhad Air Base on one of our programs they're using there. Why are you here? And in a frigging harem?"

She pulled back so her gaze met his. "I can't say."

Matt frowned. He had almost the highest clearance there was. She should realize that. "You don't know if you can trust me?"

Sam leaned close again. "I do know that you're going to blow my cover if you don't start playing the part of the horny American with the harem girl."

He knew she was right, but that still didn't make it feel less strange or less wrong. Or less disturbingly good as she reached between them and wrapped her fingers around his cock.

She stroked him again. Her tongue tickled his ear, sending a shiver down his spine.

"Do you know they think you're gay?" She drew in a sharp breath and pulled away. "Are you?"

"No." The evidence to the contrary sat heavy in her hand.

"It's okay if you—"

"Sam. No. I'm not." He slid one hand down to cup her ass as he gripped her chin with the other.

Smashing his lips into hers, he kissed her deep and hard. It was as much to prove his point as it was because he wanted to. And, of course, he also had the excuse of making things look real for surveillance.

Kissing her felt good. Too good.

Matt pulled back, more frustrated and confused than before and he hadn't thought that possible. "What do we do now?"

"Put on a show for the cameras."

His eyes opened wider. "We can't have sex."

"Why the hell not?"

"We work together."

"No, we don't. We're on different teams. In six months we've never met in person. We work so far apart that all this time you thought I was a man, for God's sake."

"But we're . . . You're . . ."

"We're supposed to do whatever necessary to maintain

security on an op. You know that." She bit her lower lip and continued, "And don't think badly of me, but I'm horny as hell. You try walking around wearing nothing but scarves all day and see if it doesn't get to you."

It already had gotten to him, even before she confessed how turned on she was.

Matt groaned, running his hands down her back. "Are you sure?"

"Yes, dammit. Now shut up and fuck me."

His buddy Sam sure had a way with words.

That was it. He was done fighting. Matt ran his hands over her smooth, slick skin, all the way down to cup her ass. He hoisted her up and pressed her against the shower wall. She wrapped her long legs around his waist.

Her arms around his neck, she grabbed his hair and steered his mouth to hers.

Matt stopped her just short of the kiss. "Birth control?"

"We're good."

She'd barely gotten the words out when Matt couldn't wait any longer. The self-deprivation of his time here caught up with him. He took her mouth and her body at the same time.

His tongue met hers while he lowered her over his erection. His tip speared her, sliding in easily.

She hadn't been lying when she said she wanted this. Sam's body accepted his like they'd been made to fit together.

He sank deeper into her with a shudder. She moaned and it was his undoing.

Matt stroked in and out a few more times before he knew he couldn't hold on. "I'm not gonna last long."

She opened her heavily lidded eyes. "We have all night. I'm supposed to stay as long as you want me."

That could be for much longer than one night.

Matt pumped fast into her, both of their breaths coming faster as he worked. As he feared, it didn't take long at all. He came, fast and hard, with one long groan.

He wasn't ready to leave her body yet, but he had to as the muscles bearing her weight started to shake and his cock faded. He eased her feet to the ground and reached between them.

Maybe he'd been a little quick out of the gate, but he was very good with his hands. He'd prove that to her. He slid his right hand between her legs. Working her clit, he watched her face.

Eyes closed, head thrown back as she leaned against the wall, she started to come undone. He didn't let up until he had her shaking and crying out. She came hard, clinging to his arms as she did. He held her as her knees buckled and she slumped breathless.

She drew in a shaky breath. "Wow."

The purely male part of Matt took great pride in her reaction. "If you liked that, wait until you see the sex toys in my bedside table. Even I don't know what some of them are for."

She laughed. "Considering you're the computer god, that's saying something. I guess we'll have to figure them out together."

That thought had him ready for another round. He turned off the water and stepped out of the stall to grab a towel. His feet slipped on the wet marble as he did.

He caught himself on the towel bar before he went down. "Shit."

Sam watched, one brow cocked up. "Don't fall and break anything I might need later."

She didn't need to worry. He'd put a splint on it if he had to, but nothing was going to get in the way of him enjoying every last second with her.

Matt formulated his plan. More horny-American-and-the-harem-girl sex first. After that, he'd get her to tell him why she was here.

He'd help her complete her assignment and get her the hell out of there. Undercover mission or not, he hated the idea of her being here.

A harem. What the hell was her commander thinking? He was going to make it his business to get her out and fast.

CHAPTER NINE

Lying naked on her belly, Sam glanced into the drawer in the bedside table. The array of sex toys inside was mind-boggling.

Apparently what she'd read and been told about modern day harems was bullshit. At least in this palace. These women were not here as window dressing, pretty things to look at.

This place was equipped to be a sexual pleasure dome, and she was smack in the middle of it.

"What do you think this one is for?" Next to her, Matt held up a small black acorn-shaped object. "It looks a little like a pacifier for a baby. Is it for playing naughty nursemaid and bad boy who needs to be spanked?"

He raised the item in question toward his lips. Sam grabbed his wrist. "Ah, I wouldn't do that if I were you. It's definitely not a pacifier. It's a butt plug."

She laughed out loud at the expression on Matt's face—a mix of shock and intrigue as his golden-brown eyes opened wide.

"Really? Hmm." Sandy-colored eyebrows raised, he considered the item in his hand again and then reached into the drawer and pulled out a tube of lubricant. "I guess this goes with that."

The wheels in Matt's brain were turning. Sam could tell he

was planning something and it probably involved the two items in his hands and her.

Time to shake him up a bit.

She leaned in and nipped his earlobe. "Definitely. Don't you worry. I'll use plenty of lube on that plug before I stick it in you."

He opened his mouth before he closed it again and swallowed.

"No comment?" she asked.

"None at the moment." Matt cleared his throat. After putting the lube and plug down, he glanced into the drawer again. He pulled out a curved T-shaped toy with a ball at one end and a bulbous center. "Okay, since you seem to be the expert, what is this?"

Sam wasn't untrained in the world of sex toys. She'd been single too long to not know everything that was available on her favorite site.

It's amazing what a person could find on the internet. She was well versed in the world of sexual devices, including the proper use of the prostate massager Matt held in his hand.

She smiled. "Want me to show you?"

He looked at the shape and length of it. "I don't know. I think that depends. Is it for me or for you?"

"Oh, it's unquestionably for you." She laughed.

He shook his head. "Then no. I don't want you to show me. Just tell me."

"You sure? It's supposed to be pretty amazing. Best male orgasms ever."

"From this? Nope, I don't think so. How?"

"How? Well, it's a prostate massager, so you should be able to guess how." She laughed as Matt cringed.

He looked at it one more time and put it back in the drawer as if he never wished to touch it again. "You're scaring me."

"Don't worry. I promise to be gentle."

Matt frowned. "How do you know about all this stuff?"

She wasn't about to tell him it was from sexual frustration

and a teeny addiction to internet porn, so she said, "Just part of the job description for a harem girl."

She figured they could speak freely and not worry about the surveillance as long as they stuck to topics like sex. If they needed to speak about anything regarding her assignment, they'd have to take another shower to cover the conversation.

They couldn't do that too often. Eventually, whoever was watching would get suspicious. Or maybe not . . . Matt pulled a bottle of massage oil from the drawer full of goodies. He poured a good amount into his hand and grinned. It looked as if they were about to get messy, after which they'd need another shower.

"Roll over." He leaned low over her back and slipped his tongue around the whorls of her ear. "That butt plug thing. Is that just for men or can I use it on you?"

Matt might be a computer genius, the best of the best in their field, but it seemed there were a few things Sam could teach him in the sexual arena.

"You can use it on me." The thought had her heart beating faster and the muscles low in her belly clenching.

They had tonight, but her mission hung over her. Maybe she would tell him about her assignment.

If she enlisted Matt's help, and if he lived up to his reputation, he could figure out a way to find the source of the signal. He definitely could move around the compound more freely than she could.

She'd have to warn him not to use the computer provided for him for anything other than playing games. It was definitely not secure—but of course, he would have figured that out already.

Her thought process wasn't working up to speed. Not her fault. It was hard to think as Matt slipped his oiled hands down her back and over the naked skin of her ass.

The sensations bombarding her made it difficult to concentrate on work.

She should be concerned with the mission and her cover. That someone might notice she was acting awfully friendly with an American military man. But when he delved his slick fingers between her butt cheeks and pressed against her hole, she accepted that she wouldn't be able to think about anything else for a little while.

Matt moved to kneel between her spread legs. "Mmm. I'm really glad you brought me my dinner tray."

Sam laughed. "You didn't eat any of it."

"I'll get to it. I plan on getting to lots of things before tonight is over." He ran both hands down her spine.

The shaky breath she drew in when his slick fingertip breached her entrance had him leaning low to say, "Tell me if I hurt you."

His breath against her ear sent a shiver through her. "You're not hurting me."

He moaned, soft and low near her ear and pushed in deeper. "Good."

Yes, it was. Very good.

CHAPTER TEN

Head bowed over the keyboard, Matt watched the screen while his fingers flew across the keys.

Sam had finally spilled her assignment to him during their second shower together last night.

It didn't take Matt long to formulate a plan. While lathering Sam's incredibly hot body with his hands, he'd whispered his idea to her under the cover of the sound of the water. She'd agreed.

He'd gone to the air base early that morning. In actuality, he was done with them, but their base offered a secure computer and a good excuse for him to still be here as he pretended to his palace hosts he had more work to do.

At the base, he created a program that looked real but wasn't. Back at his room, Matt proceeded as if he had more work to do that he hadn't gotten done on site.

He loaded the program he'd created onto the computer in his room. The trick was he'd rigged it so it appeared to work, but in reality it had very limited functionality. Then he added what he thought was an absolute stroke of genius—an invisible tracking program.

Now he worked like a fiend on the computer provided for him in his room. The same computer he and Sam both believed was not by any stretch of the imagination secure.

He knew that any bad guy hoping to steal American military technology or secrets would access anything Matt did here, and that was his plan exactly.

Whoever was contacting known terrorists from within this compound would hopefully find the program Matt had planted.

If they did, they would definitely forward the technology and inadvertently lead the good guys to them. That way, instead of just capturing the one fish Sam had been sent to locate, they'd get the whole pond full. Everyone and anyone connected.

It was no small task to code all of this on the fly, but Matt thrived on pressure.

In fact, he didn't notice the sun set and ignored the growling in his stomach until a knock on the door reminded him that Sam should be delivering his evening meal.

He glanced at his watch.

She was late. He could definitely stand a meal break . . . and a sex break.

He flung open the door, intending to tease her about being a bad little harem girl for delivering her master's meal late, but Rashid stood in the doorway, tray in hand.

Matt stepped back into the room. "Rashid. Where's . . ."

What name was she using? They'd gotten around to a lot the night before, but the name she'd given them at the compound wasn't one of them.

"Uh, the girl who was here last night? Blue eyes, short light hair, pretty . . ."

"You mean Sabrina." Rashid frowned. "You like her, I can see. But I have bad news."

Matt's heart pounded harder. "What bad news?"

"She was taken away today."

He braced himself with one hand on the edge of the desk and tried to cover his panic.

Hoping his voice didn't betray his feelings, he asked, "What do you mean taken?"

"A man came and said she belonged to him. That she had

run from him and he was here to take her back. Then he hit her. Hard. I saw blood on her mouth."

Matt swallowed the bile that rose in his throat. "Thank you, Rashid. You can go. I have work to do."

Rashid bowed his head and backed out of the room. Matt managed to wait for the door to close before he collapsed in the computer chair.

His mind raced. Of course, she wasn't a runaway. Was this her cover story and all part of her exfil? But wouldn't she have waited to make sure the program he was working on was a success before she left?

What was to stop any random man from claiming her as his own? In this part of the world, authorities would take a man's word over a woman's every day.

His stomach clenched.

He closed his eyes and drew in a deep breath. He was nearly finished with the installation. A little more time, if he could get his brain to focus on the job and not Sam, and he'd be done.

But there was still no way he could search for her in Dubai. It would raise suspicion. Besides, she might not even still be in Dubai.

Matt had to have faith in her to take care of herself. Faith in Omega team to take care of her, just as Zeta took care of their own.

Easier said than done.

He flashed back to the condition Jimmy had been in by the time they'd extracted him after his cover had been blown.

That didn't help calm his nerves. Exactly the opposite.

The best thing he could do to help her was finish planting the bait and then get his ass out of this place so he could find out what happened to Sam.

First thing he'd do once he was clear of here and could contact the commander securely, was pass on all that had happened. Central Command could get her location from her tracking device.

Hopefully, a call to Omega would yield the information

Matt wanted—that Sam was en route to the States—safe and sound.

If not, he'd track down both her and whomever she was with, and God help the man who took her.

Flinging open the door, Matt turned to the ever-present guard. "I need transportation to the airport. Who do I talk to about that?"

CHAPTER ELEVEN

As she watched the scenery whiz by the car window, Sam fingered her throbbing mouth.

The cut on her fat lip was going to look even prettier by tomorrow when it was set off by all the colors her bruise would turn.

She picked up the ice pack and held it in place, wondering if her mouth hurt more with or without the cold pressed to it. But the sick feeling in her gut wasn't from being hit. It was because every minute, every mile, took her farther away from Matt.

Was he still in the compound? Had he been able to code the Trojan Horse program they'd talked about? And if so, did he get away clean afterward?

If anyone figured out what he was up to, they could have detained him—or worse.

A large male hand covered hers. "Foster, I'm so sorry."

"Please, sir. Stop apologizing. Just try and remember the next time you get into playing the role of angry harem-girl master, wear the gaudy gold ring on your left hand and make sure you slap me with your right." She winced as speaking opened the crack in her lip wider.

"I hope there isn't a next time." His eyes focused on the road as he drove, Commander Anderson drew in a deep breath and shook his head. "But if there is, check in when you're supposed to so I don't assume you've been compromised."

If one of the guys on the team had gone dark for a few days during an undercover op, the commander wouldn't have come swooping in like a deranged Superman and dragged them out.

Sam scowled at the double standard. "It was too risky to contact you. I had no privacy whatsoever."

In hindsight, she should have had Matt make contact for her, but that wouldn't have been without its risks either, for both of them.

Her commander should have trusted in her skills. He hadn't and that pissed Sam off. Instead, he'd swept in wearing a disguise so over the top it nearly made her laugh.

But he'd spewed Farsi like he'd been born speaking it, and had no problem convincing everyone there what he spoke was the truth. His pretend anger over Sam's presence there had even the guards cowering, especially after he added a backhanded blow across her mouth.

He demanded his property—that being her—be returned and Sam and her single bag had been handed over to him immediately.

Commander Anderson looked in her direction again and cringed. "Good thing you don't have some big protective boyfriend around, huh? He'd kick my ass for what I did to your face."

"Yeah. Good thing." Her mind turned to Matt once again. Their brief time together. The feel of his hands on her. She wouldn't mind having a big protective boyfriend. Not one bit.

Her commander slowed the car to a stop at the security checkpoint at their Virginia base's front gate. He glanced at her as the guard checked his ID, saluted and waved the vehicle through. "You up for this? The debriefing can wait a day. You can skip the team meeting. Take a few days if you need to."

Sam frowned. "Are you kidding? I finally got a battle scar.

There's no way I'm hiding at home and not showing it off to the guys."

That earned her a smile from Commander Anderson. "All right. Understood. I'll stop coddling you. You handled yourself well, Foster."

"Thanks, but the program to monitor and track the transmissions was Matt Coleman's doing, not mine." Sam had waited a long time for a compliment like that from her leader, but she had to give credit where credit was due.

"I think you would have come up with something on your own, but I'm glad he was there because I don't want to even think about what you would have had to resort to if he hadn't been."

That thought had crossed Sam's mind too. Cozying up to the Brunei prince was the last thing she'd wanted to do, but she would have done it to gain information.

On the other hand, playing harem girl with Matt hadn't been a hardship at all. Her insides heated just thinking about him, even as her concern for his wellbeing hung over her.

First chance she had, she was going to try and contact him.

The commander parked the car in the lot nearest their building. "Last chance. You want to go home and rest? We just got off the plane—"

Sam cocked a brow. "Commander, if I needed to run home and nap every time I lost a little sleep, I'm in the wrong profession."

"All right. Your choice." He swung open the door and stepped out, glancing at her over the hood of the black SUV. "Meeting at zero-eight-hundred."

"Perfect. Just enough time for me to microwave a cup of tea first."

"Whatever floats your boat." He shook his head and smiled.

Commander Anderson didn't believe Sam's claim that tea had as much caffeine as coffee, but he didn't argue with her about it now the way he usually did. More proof of his guilty conscience over her fat lip.

A quarter of an hour later, Sam sat at the table surrounded by the members of Omega.

Her teammate Justin eyed her from across the table. "Nice lip."

"Thanks." She sipped gingerly from her steaming mug, trying not to inflict more pain on herself.

Next to her, Glenn leaned close. "How was the harem?"

"Sorry, but what happens in the harem, stays in the harem." She couldn't help but smile at his raised brow. That hurt, but was worth it.

The commander stepped out of his office and into the meeting room, ending further interrogation by her team.

"I just got off the phone with Commander Miller from Task Force Zeta. Foster worked with Zeta's communications officer in Dubai and the program they put in place has already tracked the transmission to its destination. No surprise, it went directly to a heavily guarded compound located in Pakistan, which we believe to be occupied by leaders of Al Qaeda."

A wide grin spread across Sam's face. It made her lip hurt like hell, but she couldn't help it.

This was huge news. It meant that not only had Matt gotten the program up and running, but it had yielded the exact results they'd hoped for. What it didn't answer was if Matt had gotten out safely. That thought erased her smile.

"Are we going in, sir?" Justin leaned forward, looking excited at the hope of some action.

"Not yet." The commander's answer wasn't a surprise.

Central Command would want to watch and wait to see where else Matt's tracking device might lead before going in and tipping their hand.

At least, that's what she would do if the decision were up to her. Of course, if Sam were in charge, she would also have already been on the phone to Commander Miller demanding to know if Matt was safe.

The meeting room door flung open, smashing against the

wall and interrupting further thought. Every gaze inside turned, including Sam's. What she saw overwhelmed her.

Matt stood in the doorway. He took one look at her and let out a huge breath. His relief at seeing her was clear in his expression. He must have been crazed when she disappeared from the compound.

She stood, but it was the commander who spoke first. "May I help you?"

Sam swallowed and tried to keep her voice calm as she said, "Commander Anderson, this is Zeta's comm officer Matt Coleman. He was in Dubai helping me."

The commander looked from her to Matt. Sam could only imagine how relieved she looked at seeing Matt safe.

"Well, then. We owe you thanks. That was a brilliant plan."

Matt tore his gaze away from her to address the commander. "Thank you, sir."

"Sir, I haven't had a follow-up report from Coleman yet. Could I be excused from the meeting, obtain the report and then relay it to you?"

Sam was shaking. He'd come to find her. To get here so soon, he must have flown directly to Virginia from Dubai instead of going back to his own base in North Carolina.

"Go ahead, Foster." The commander almost controlled his smile, but not quite. "Take all the time you need."

"Thank you, sir." She ignored the team as they stared. She didn't react as one guy snickered.

Maybe it was obvious more had gone on in Dubai than just coding a program, but she didn't give a crap what they thought.

Sam led Matt out the door, down the hall and into an empty office. She managed to not attack him until they were alone, but then she didn't hold back.

Throwing her arms around his neck, she ignored her swollen lip and kissed him hard, until the pain of her cut had her pulling back. Still she couldn't bear to break all contact, so she hugged him tighter.

Matt held her close and buried his face in her hair. "I was so worried."

"I'm sorry. The commander pulled me out sooner than I'd planned or I would have told you."

"It's all right. You're safe. That's all that matters." He ran his hands over her as if looking for more injuries. His gaze settled on her lip. "Did he really have to hit you to get you out of there?"

"He and I have already discussed that. I'm fine. Tell me what happened after I left."

"I loaded the program on the computer in the room, made a few bullshit changes to look as if I was working on it—"

"Hoping every keystroke would be recorded and then used by the leak," Sam added.

"Exactly." Matt nodded. "Then I heard you'd been taken and I hopped on the first flight I could get."

Sam smiled. "To my base, not to yours."

"I had to see for myself that you were here and all right." He squeezed her tighter. "Please, tell me you're not going undercover again anytime soon."

She returned his hug, loving how concerned he was. "Not that I know of."

Matt pulled back enough to cup her face. He leaned in and kissed just the good corner of her mouth. "I have to admit, I do hope that you kept the harem girl outfit."

"Perv." She laughed. "And yes, I did, since I was wearing it when the commander dragged me out."

"Perv, huh?" Matt looked devilish. "After that, I guess I shouldn't tell you that I emptied the sex toy drawer into my bag before I left."

Her eyes opened wide. "You didn't."

"I sure as hell did." He smirked. "I almost had to abandon my running shoes there to be able to zip the bag. I think it's going to take us quite a bit of time to get through trying them all."

"I look forward to it." She smiled until reality crept in. "Can you stay? Or do you have to get right back?"

"I've got at least tonight. I'm hoping tomorrow night too. I have to check with my commander."

One night, even two, wasn't going to be enough time. "How's this going to work, Matt?"

"Us?" he asked.

Us. Sam liked the sound of that, but she couldn't figure out how they could be an *us* if they were stationed in two different states.

She nodded.

He shrugged. "We'll see each other whenever we can."

"And when we can't?" she asked.

"I'll send you naughty instant messages. And there's always video chat." He ran a thumb over her cheek. "Between the two of us, we'll figure something out. I'll move heaven and earth to spend time with you."

To her horror, his sweet words brought tears to her eyes. "Dammit, Coleman. You made me cry like a damn woman."

A smile lit Matt's face. "You are a woman and have I told you how immensely grateful I am for that?"

"I'm pretty grateful for it myself." She flicked away a tear and realized she could love this man. Hell, she suspected she already did.

"Now that I finally know my good buddy Sam Foster is not a man, I have every intention of taking full advantage of that fact."

"I have every intention of letting you." She leaned in but stopped just shy of his lips. "Did you take the prostate massager too?"

His cheeks flushed as he momentarily broke eye contact, making him look even more adorable. "Yes."

Sam smiled. "Good."

Maybe she would take the commander up on his offer of time off.

Getting through the contents of Matt's bag could take days. But getting enough of Matt Coleman might take more than one lifetime.

THE COMMANDER

CHAPTER ONE

"Commander?"

Hank Miller glanced up from the stack of papers and folders on his desk to see Jimmy Gordon, one of Task Force Zeta's team members, hovering in the doorway. "What's up, Gordon?"

"We're fixin' to head on over to the bar. You coming?"

Jimmy's thick-as-molasses Southern drawl had the New Jersey–native inside Hank smiling, but the invitation out tonight? Not so much.

It had been a long time since Hank had been young, single and energetic enough to think going out after a full day of work was fun.

Now, in his forties, divorced and tired, Hank looked forward to going one place when his day was done. Home.

In SpecOps, their workday could literally last thirty-six hours, depending on the mission.

In comparison, today had been easy. Some training exercises followed by this never-ending stack of mind-numbing paperwork that Hank found far more exhausting than a good hard workout with the team.

"Thanks for the invite, but I was going to finish up with this crap, then head home and crash."

"Understood, but could you come for a few minutes? You don't have to stay, but I'd like to talk to y'all together."

"Hey, hey, hey. Wait one minute." Matt Coleman leaned in the doorway, some kind of gadget in his hand. The man was like a walking computer store. Hank had long ago stopped trying to keep up with his new toys. "I agreed to going out for a beer, but no one said anything about having a team meeting tonight."

Jimmy frowned at Matt. "It's not a team meeting."

"Fine. Tell me when we're leaving." Matt ducked out again as abruptly as he'd arrived, leaving Jimmy still waiting for Hank's answer.

"You sure you want to talk at the bar, Gordon? Wouldn't you rather discuss whatever this is at the meeting in the morning?"

"No, sir. It's not work related. It's . . . personal."

"All right." The stack of paperwork Hank had no inspiration to finish was as much a factor in his decision as Jimmy's intriguing summons. "One beer, a quick talk and then I'm outta there."

Jimmy smiled. "Thank you, sir. Trey and Jack are there already. I'm heading over now with the rest of the guys. We'll wait for you."

On the short drive to the bar just outside the base's back gate, Hank considered what Jimmy was so anxious to discuss that it required the whole team assemble for it.

A few possibilities came to mind, none of which he liked very much. He could only hope Jimmy wasn't about to announce his leaving the military, or that he was leaving the team.

Group dynamics could be a tricky thing. Hank had recently recruited and added a new team member. So far, John Blake had worked out fine, but it could have just as easily gone the other way.

He'd hate to make another change so soon—about as much as he hated the thought of losing a valuable senior operator like Jimmy.

Inside the bar, Hank's men surrounded two tables they'd pushed together. As he made his way back to them, he saw

Trey Williams headed in the same direction with two hands filled with bottles of beer.

It wasn't totally a bad thing that Trey had started dating the woman who owned the bar. Carly made sure they got good service whenever they were here. Unfortunately, it also meant the team was at the bar even more often than they used to be.

When everyone was settled and as quiet as they were going to get, Jimmy stood. "Y'all know I'm not real good at speeches, but I've got something important to announce."

This sounded serious, which made the chances of Hank liking whatever Jimmy was about to say slim to none.

"Well, I *am* good at speeches, big brother." Bottle poised in one hand, Jack Gordon looked up at Jimmy. "Let me tell 'em."

"Don't you dare. I can do this my own damn self." After glaring at Jack, Jimmy paused long enough to draw a deep breath. "Lia and I are getting married and I want all y'all to stand up with me at the ceremony."

No retirement announcement. No plans to quit the team. Just a wedding. That, Hank could handle. "Congratulations, Gordon. It would be an honor to stand with you at the altar."

"Congratulations, buddy." Bull stood and slapped Jimmy on the back with enough force it knocked Jimmy a step forward.

"Congrats, man. When are you gonna take the plunge?" John asked.

"Um, well that's the thing." Jimmy cringed and glanced at the group. "It's next weekend."

"Next weekend?" Trey planted his bottle on the table with a clunk. "Jeez, Jimmy. What the hell. Why so soon? You knock her up or something?"

All eyes focused on Jimmy. His silence answered the question as Hank began to suspect Trey had hit the nail right on the head.

Jack grinned. "Yup. I'm gonna be an uncle."

Some of these guys seemed so damn young that there had

been times Hank felt more like a father to them than a commander. Now they were having kids of their own.

What did that make Hank? He didn't even want to think the word grandfather. Which reminded him, he needed to call his daughter.

It had been far too long since he'd spoken with his only child. Thank God, she wasn't married or even talking about it yet. Hopefully he had some time left before he really became a grandfather.

Jimmy shot Jack a less-than-happy look. "Thanks a lot, Jack."

"They would have noticed eventually. Lia's tits are getting huge." Jack held one palm out in front of his chest. "Her belly is gonna follow shortly."

The punch Jimmy delivered to Jack's arm splashed the beer in his hand all over the table. "Keep your mouth shut and your eyes off her chest."

"Easier said than done. I mean holy shit, she's—" Jack never finished his ill-advised observation as Jimmy dove at him. Bull and BB Dalton were up just as fast, each one grabbing a Gordon brother.

It could be a hairy situation when men trained to kill with their bare hands got into a bar fight, but Hank figured the Gordon boys had been scrapping with each other their entire lives.

Not to mention there were half a dozen men here trained just as well to break them up. Hank could afford to sit back and relax for this one. It might be because he was tired and bored as shit even thinking of that paperwork on his desk, but he found the two brothers bickering amusing.

Bull, still holding on to Jimmy, eyed him. "You gonna calm down so I can finish my beer?"

Jimmy scowled one more time in Jack's direction, then nodded.

"Jack? You done?" BB asked.

"I didn't start it."

"Are. You. Done." BB's tone left no question he'd had

enough with Jack being a smart ass.

Jack scowled. "Yeah, I'm done."

"Fine." BB released his hold and sat. "And congratulations, Jimmy. I'm happy for you. I'm sure every one of us would be honored to stand up with you."

"Of course, we all will. As long as we don't get assigned between now and then." Matt pointed out the one glitch that could sink the whole plan.

The team could be called out on a moment's notice, unless Hank did something to avoid it.

"Where are you having the ceremony?" Hank asked.

"I want to have it at my mama's."

"In Pigeon Hollow?" Trey laughed. "Does Lia's daddy, the state governor, know his only daughter's getting married on a horse farm?"

Jack snorted. "I, for one, don't give a flying crap what the governor thinks. He should be proud to have his daughter married to a Gordon and at our home to boot."

Jimmy ignored Jack. "Lia and I discussed it with him and he's fine with it."

"Really? Hmm." Hank considered that tidbit as interesting as it was odd.

"Remember, he's all into supporting the small farmer." Jimmy scowled. "He thinks it's good press for us to get married at the farm."

"And he's all right with, you know, the little Jimmy on the way?" Bull asked.

Jimmy treated them to his crooked grin. "With a little one on the way, he'd much rather have us married than not."

"Matt made a good point, though. For once." Jack tipped a bottle to Matt in a salute. "What if we get called out on an assignment between now and then? What do we do?"

The team turned toward Hank for an answer. Luckily, he had one. "Well, boys. I say it's time we turn Central Command's asinine rules right back on them."

"I sure do like the sound of that." Jack grinned. "What do you have in mind, sir?"

"Remember when they forced us all to take furlough—what they called mental-health leave—because none of us was using our time off?" Just remembering how command had tried to tell him how to run his team pissed Hank off.

Jack let out a short laugh. "How can I forget?"

Trey and Matt exchanged a look and Hank shot them all a warning glance. "I think we best not discuss that right now."

Hank knew damn well Jack had done some shit he shouldn't have during that leave, and that Jimmy, Trey and Matt had joined him for it.

He'd long since decided when it came to this particular situation, what he didn't know, couldn't hurt him. Particularly since what Hank did know was that four of his team had conveniently converged in Pigeon Hollow just hours before a mysterious tip led the feds to evidence that landed an infamous mobster in jail.

Matt, the one man in this group most likely able to hack into the mob's computer, send the files to the FBI and not leave a trail, raised his longneck bottle in a toast. "Yes, sir."

Hank turned the subject back to safer territory. "Anyway. I propose, if you are all agreeable, that we use a few of our accrued days to go to Pigeon Hollow for the wedding. Central can't complain. It's their damn rule that we can't travel out of range unless on assignment or official leave. They'll just force us to take it some other time if we don't use it."

"I'm fine with that." Matt nodded. "Vote? All in favor?"

There was a collective response of, "Aye."

"All right. I'll put us all in for it effective tomorrow on my way home." This was one bit of paperwork Hank wouldn't mind doing.

"Thank you, sir." Jimmy's gaze shifted from Hank to the rest of the team. "Y'all being there means a lot."

"Wouldn't miss it for the world, Gordon. Besides, I can finally meet the famous Mama and taste her prize-winning sweet-potato pie you're always bragging about." Hank grinned.

Jimmy laughed. "I'd love to have you meet her, sir. Knowing Mama, I'm sure there'll be more pie than any of us can eat."

Hank took one last sip to empty the bottle and rose. "If that's all for the announcement, then I'm heading out."

"I'll walk out with you, sir. I don't want Lia to worry."

"Whipped already and you haven't even said *I do* yet." Matt shook his head.

"Jealous?" Jimmy's brow rose.

"Damn right, I am. My girlfriend's in a different country right now. And let's not forget I was on the comm unit and heard you and Lia going at it the night you met her. It sounded pretty—"

Hank braced himself, expecting to have to hold Jimmy back before he pummeled Matt. "Watch it, Coleman. She's the mother of his child and about to become his wife."

Jimmy didn't lunge. He just shook his head. "You're a dick, Matt."

Maybe fatherhood would mellow the man.

Not acting as smart as he was, Matt continued, "Come on, sir. You heard it too. You have to admit—"

"Zip it, Coleman." Hank's tone was stern enough to convey to Matt that he should shut the fuck up.

"Yes, sir." Matt sighed.

Sometimes it was good to be in charge. His duty done, Hank threw a five-dollar bill down on the table for his beer and said, "Good night, all. Anyone who comes in tomorrow morning with a hangover gets an extra ten miles on the course."

Jack frowned. "I thought our leave started tomorrow."

"Oh, it does. At twelve-hundred, *after* our workout." Hank smiled as grumbling followed him and Jimmy to the exit where they pushed through the door to the parking lot.

Hank decided to feel Jimmy out a bit while he had him alone. "You all right with this happening so fast, Gordon?"

The parking-lot light illuminated Jimmy's face enough Hank could see him beaming with a smile. "I'm thrilled. I'm more than ready to be married to Lia. She was so busy running her father's political career, she wasn't in any rush to make things permanent. The baby changed that."

As they reached his car, a suspicion struck Hank. "You didn't—"

"Get her pregnant on purpose? No. But it sure worked out in the end. I'm in my thirties. I'm ready. And now she has to marry me." Jimmy grinned wider.

"Our line of work is tough on a marriage, son. You better be prepared for that." Hank didn't want to butt in, but their discussion was already about as personal as it could get.

"We've been together for quite a while now. Lia knows what to expect."

"A baby might change things." That was one thing Hank knew too well.

Jimmy shrugged. "Then we'll have to cross that bridge when we come to it."

"All right." Hank had done all he could. "So, what day does Zeta descend upon the unsuspecting town of Pigeon Hollow?"

CHAPTER TWO

The ringing of the phone stopped Lois Gordon midway between the laundry room and the bedroom. Over the pile of sheets in her arms, she glanced at the caller ID on the readout of the hallway phone.

Juggling the pile of laundry, she grabbed the cordless receiver and managed to hit the button to answer. "Jimmy. Hey, darlin'."

"Hey, Mama."

"Where you at?" Dumping the pile of sheets onto her absent middle son's mattress, Lois forced herself to sit down amid the chaos so she could concentrate on talking to her eldest.

It seemed as if ever since he'd sprung this wedding on her, she'd been spinning in circles. Hosting a wedding at the farm with two weeks' notice, and with the governor and his high falutin' friends as guests, was crazy.

"In the car with Lia on our way there. The team's following behind me."

She blew out a slow breath and attempted to sound upbeat. "Great."

Lois shoved her hand through her hair to get it off her face. Between the weather and the stress she was tempted to tear it all out. She rolled the hairband off her wrist and twisted it around a quick, messy ponytail while trying to cradle the receiver on one shoulder.

The pressure was starting to get to her. Jimmy would never know it. Neither would the guests. Her mama had raised her right. By the time everyone arrived, the house would be perfect and the food would be ready.

But until then, inside, she'd allow herself a small amount of panic.

She'd already calculated how many she could accommodate in the house. As much as she hated it, the rest would have to make do in the empty apartment above the barn. "I hope your friends won't mind doubling up in the beds."

"No worries, Mama. I called the Hideaway and reserved a bunch of rooms. You'll probably only have to deal with Lia and me at the house. Maybe Jack unless he's staying with Nicki at her dad's place."

"You didn't have to get them hotel rooms. It'll be tight, but they're all welcome here." Lois had never turned away a guest in need of a place to sleep and she never would.

He laughed. "Yeah, I did. It's just easier this way. The guys all have girlfriends now. I told them there's a strict no-sharing-a-room-before-marriage policy under your roof."

"As it should be." Lois didn't tell Jimmy her policy had fallen by the wayside with Jared getting a girlfriend of his own.

When Mandy was in town and not traveling for business, she was practically moved in to Jared's room.

The boy was old enough now. He could make his own decisions. She couldn't reprimand him like he was a teenager. Jared was the man of the house with his two older brothers away.

"Yes, Mama." There was a smile in Jimmy's voice.

It took great restraint to not remind Jimmy that his living under the same roof with Lia before marriage had led to Lois becoming a grandmother and this quickie wedding.

It wasn't like she was a prude. Far from it. She wasn't

under any delusion that her sons weren't going to have sex at their ages, but she wasn't even fifty yet. That was too damn young to have someone calling her grandma, in her opinion.

Even if she didn't have a sex life or a man, she didn't need the label of *grandma* slapped on her making her feel old or like her life was done.

Lois shook that morbid thought away and got back to the matter at hand.

"How many people are coming with you?" She glanced at the clock.

If they didn't speed, which she knew they would, they'd be here in about two hours. She needed to get these beds made, check on the ribs slow-cooking in the oven and see to some last-minute details for tonight's party for Lia.

She looked down at herself. Changing into something that didn't make her look like a farmhand should probably be on her list at some point as well.

"Let's see, there's me, Lia, the commander, Matt, but he's alone since his girl can't make it, Bull, his girl is coming but not until tomorrow, Jack of course, Trey and Carly, BB and Katie and their new baby. Oh, and the new guy John and his girl, but she's driving out with Bull's girlfriend. How many is that?"

"Thirteen." Lois ran out of fingers on her two hands. That wasn't counting the infant he'd mentioned and all the folks already in Pigeon Hollow—Jack's girlfriend Nicki, and Jared and his girlfriend Mandy.

"You bake a pie today, Mama?" Jimmy asked. "The commander is looking forward to tasting what I've been boasting about for years."

"Yes, darlin', I made a pie." Lucky for Jimmy, she'd baked six. Jesus wasn't here to turn her water into wine or make one pie serve the more than dozen people Jimmy had brought with him.

Good thing Lois knew better than to bank on what her sons told her. He'd originally said today's visitors would be just his teammates.

Lois hadn't thought to ask about girlfriends. Last she'd heard they'd all been single and looking.

Leave it to a man to totally forget they'd all want to bring their girls for the weekend. But Lois loved her three sons, every blessed one of them. Good thing too, because there were times when she wanted to strangle them.

CHAPTER THREE

The convoy of vehicles had hit the highway an hour later than planned, but at least now they were almost to their destination—Pigeon Hollow, North Carolina.

The government-issue black SUV driven by Jack, with Hank riding shotgun, also contained Bull and Matt, along with John Blake, the team's various dress uniforms and one wedding dress.

A convertible sports car holding the bride and groom led the way.

Bull's girl had to work tonight so she'd drive down tomorrow with Blake's girlfriend. BB's SUV with Katie and the baby brought up the rear, behind Trey's pickup truck that he drove with Carly.

It had been like staging a damn mission to get everybody in one place and ready to leave. Hank liked when things were organized and on schedule. Today's departure had been enough to raise his blood pressure.

Some needed to fuel up. Others needed to hit the drive-thru for something to eat. If Hank's hair hadn't gone gray years ago, this trip might have done it. Coordinating a team was one thing. This jumbled group was quite another.

Ahead of them, the convertible driven by Jimmy turned off the interstate.

"Just a few more miles now, and I do wish that brother of mine would use the damn blinker when he's driving my car." Jack scowled.

Bull laughed. "I think he's got a few other things on his mind right now, Jack."

Jack flicked on the blinker and slowed for the exit. "Yeah? Well, driving should be one of them, especially since I was nice enough to let him and the blushing bride take my car. Though with her morning sickness—actually more like all-day-long sickness—it's safer for everyone in here that she's riding in a convertible with lots of fresh air."

"Very true." Hank was very grateful to not have to deal with the threat of vomit in the vehicle he had to spend two hours in.

He'd been through morning sickness with his ex-wife many years ago. Once had been enough for him.

Hank glanced at the side mirror to make sure Trey and BB's vehicles still followed and had turned off behind them.

Ahead, the interstate changed into a two-lane road.

After a mile or two, that changed from rural nothingness to a populated small town. In the blink of an eye, they were in downtown Pigeon Hollow. At least, that's what the welcome sign said.

"So, Jack. When you gonna make an honest woman out of your girlfriend?" Bull kicked the back of Jack's seat.

"None of your business, that's when." Jack frowned at the windshield ahead.

"What's the wait? Shit. You're not still into Carly, are you?" Matt asked Jack from the back seat.

"Hell no, I'm not."

"Wait?" Blake leaned forward between the seats. "Jack used to be with Trey's girlfriend Carly?"

"No. I wasn't." Jack's grip on the steering wheel tightened.

"It was a valid question. Otherwise why wouldn't you want to marry Nicki?" Matt's comment had Jack clenching his jaw. "You've been with her longer than Lia's been with your brother, so what's the hold up?"

Hank decided he'd better intervene before Jack ended up driving off the road and wrapping them around a phone pole. "Jack, you don't have to answer. Coleman, shut the fuck up. Blake, leave history in the past where it belongs."

"It's okay, Commander. I wanna answer. Matt, not that it's any of your concern, but I'm not sure I wanna get married. Unlike my little brother Jared who's chomping at the bit to marry his girl, I'm old enough to remember when our parents were still together." Jack let out a short laugh. "I can tell you, it wasn't good."

"But Jimmy's old enough to remember that too and he's getting married," Bull pointed out.

"Jimmy got Lia pregnant." Jack cocked a brow.

Hank turned in his seat to face the man next to him. "Jack, not all marriages are created equal. Yours won't be like your parents' because you're not like your father. Neither is Jimmy."

Jack swallowed. "Thanks, Commander. And to answer your question, Blake, Carly and I had exactly one dinner date before she and Trey starting going out. End of story. Right, Matt?"

"Uh, yup. That's how it happened." For once, Matt did the smart thing. He agreed with Jack and kept his smart-ass comments—and the rest of what had happened between Trey, Carly and Jack during the Kosovo op—to himself.

"Crap, look at Jimmy now. He's speeding through town like a bull charging toward a herd of heifers," Jack shook his head and all was back to normal.

Jack continued, "And there's Bobby Barton's deputy sheriff car parked in front of the diner. Friend or not, it would serve Jimmy right if Bobby gave him a ticket. I mean, Nicki's waiting on me at the farm and it's been two weeks since I've plowed her field, but you don't see me kicking into a gallop in the middle of town, now do you?"

Matt barked out a laugh behind Hank at Jack's colorful commentary.

"Is everyone in your family as colorful as you, Jack?" John

Blake asked.

Jack met his gaze in the rearview mirror. "Next to Jared, I'm the calm one."

Bull shifted one more time in the cramped confines, his legs crushed behind Jack's seat in a space that didn't come near to accommodating his size. "God help us all if that's true."

Silently, Hank agreed with Bull. At least this weekend wouldn't be boring.

They were through town and turning onto a dirt road before Hank could say Pigeon Hollow.

An actual dirt road. The Jersey City native in Hank couldn't quite wrap his head around that concept.

After about a mile, Jimmy swung the convertible, sans blinker again, into a pretty magnolia-lined gravel drive marked by a large mailbox that read *Gordon Equine.*

Jack followed. "Here we are, boys. Welcome to the Gordon farmstead, home of the tastiest pies and the finest-bred horses in North Carolina."

"You're quite the spokesperson, Jack." Matt laughed. "Next time Central Command is looking for a poster boy for SpecOps recruiting, I'll suggest you."

Jack slowed the vehicle to a crawl as the tires crunched on the gravel. "Oh, hell no. I saw what they made BB wear in those ads. Get Blake to do it. He's the newest. He should have to."

"Don't worry, Blake. It was just some photos for recruiting ads . . . and then a few more pictures in his underwear." Bull grinned wide.

"Me?" Blake leaned forward. "I don't think so."

Hank turned in time to see the expression of horror on Blake's face. It was enough to make even Hank laugh.

The driveway seemed to stretch on forever, but eventually a sprawling white farmhouse came into view. It was so typically Southern, right down to the columns on the front porch, he wouldn't have been surprised if Scarlet O'Hara came through the front door.

As they drove closer, Hank could see that though Miss Scarlet wasn't in attendance, there were plenty of others here to greet them. Three females and one male emerged from a door off the side of the house.

From this distance, Hank recognized Jack's girl Nicki from her short dark curls. She visited the base pretty often.

The man who looked like a younger version of Jimmy and Jack must be the infamous youngest Gordon brother, Jared. He had his arm around a blonde, leading Hank to assume she was his girlfriend.

But it was the third woman who intrigued Hank most. Did Jack and Jimmy have an older sister? He didn't think so. If they did, they'd never mentioned her.

Maybe she was a cousin visiting for the wedding. Or hell, maybe the Gordons had a housekeeper. With the size of this place, they would need one.

Hank didn't care what the woman did for a living, because he was too busy admiring her denim-hugged curves.

The woman ran toward Jimmy. He swung her up and around before setting her on the ground. Then she turned to Lia and gave her a hug.

Meanwhile, Jack had already thrown the SUV into park and was out the door and hugging Nicki as fast as—what was his saying? A bull running toward some cows, or something like that. Hank was a city boy. He didn't have Jack's flair for farm talk.

He opened the passenger side door and stretched his cramped legs.

Speaking of bulls—he detected the distinct odor of shit. Horse. Cow. Chicken. Maybe a combination of all three. He wasn't sure of the origin, but it hung in the air like the stench from the refineries hung in a cloud over parts of New Jersey.

It was so pungent that Blake followed him out, sniffing the air. "What's that smell?"

"Horse manure, city boy." Matt crawled out from the third row of seats.

"The governor is going to love that being the prevailing

odor during his only daughter's wedding." Hank laughed at the thought. "I hope his friend Senator Dickson is invited so he can enjoy it too."

Bull came around from the other passenger door. "I'm sure Senator Dickhead is familiar with the stench, since he's so full of shit."

That was the truth.

Arms crossed, Hank leaned against the SUV's bumper and watched the Gordon family reunion.

Trey and Carly parked their truck next to the team vehicle, while a little farther away, BB and Katie both worked to get a sleeping baby and his car seat out of the backseat of their vehicle.

Trey stretched his arms above his head with a groan. "God, I'm stiff and I'm dying for a slice of Mrs. Gordon's pie."

Carly shot Trey a glance. "You had lunch right before we left."

"Can't blame the man, Carly. Mama Gordon's pies are amazing." Matt stared toward the group near the house. "Can you believe she's old enough to be Jimmy and Jack's mother?"

"I know." Trey shook his head. "She must have been a teenager when she had Jimmy."

The rest of the group turned to look at the woman who was now in Jack's arms.

"Wait a minute. That's Mama?" Hank nearly choked.

The hot as hell brunette in the flip-flops, blue jeans and well-filled T-shirt? The one he'd been staring at and drooling over for the past few minutes?

"Yup." Matt nodded.

"No way." Bull squinted into the distance. "I pictured her looking like Betty Crocker or Mrs. Butterworth. You know, short, plump, wearing an apron covered in flour and holding a pie in her hands."

That was how Hank had visualized her too. He certainly hadn't thought he'd be imagining rolling around sweaty with her like he'd been since he first laid eyes on the tempting woman.

"Are you sure that's Mama?" Hank couldn't wrap his mind around this revelation.

"Of course, we're sure." Trey laughed. "Matt and I were here during our leave last year."

"Visiting Jack and Jimmy," Matt added.

"Yes, I know." Hank had more productive things to worry about than what shady things these two jokers had done.

Things such as why the one woman he'd been interested in since his divorce had to be the mother of two of the men under his command. That made the situation as sticky as one of her famous pies.

Hank watched as Jimmy hustled an ill-looking Lia into the house. Jared and the blonde followed them inside with the suitcases from the trunk of the convertible and Jack escorted Mama back toward the SUV . . . and Hank.

His heart rate sped the closer she got. He smothered a curse at how his body reacted to her like he was a damn teenager.

This was the last thing he needed, a schoolboy crush on an off-limits woman.

He searched for a reason to not be attracted to Mama, besides the fact that she was Mama. He knew Jack and Jimmy's father had left when they were young. He didn't seem to be in the picture at all. Maybe Mama had a boyfriend.

A woman who looked that good wouldn't stay alone long. Yeah, that would be good. If she were dating, the guy would be invited to the wedding and then Hank wouldn't be tempted to even think about her.

He blew out a soft breath as Mama took another step toward him.

Perhaps if he kept thinking of her as Mama, he'd remember how off-limits she was. That was his plan and he was sticking to it. Though his resolve wavered as she stood in front of him.

"Commander, this is my mama, Lois Gordon," Jack

introduced them. "Mama, Commander Hank Miller."

Up close she looked even more like her sons. Like them, she had hazel eyes and golden-brown hair, except hers fell to her shoulders in soft, sun-kissed waves.

Hank extended his hand. "Mrs. Gordon, it's a pleasure to meet you. Your boys have told me so much about you."

Everything except how young and attractive she was. That bit of information would have been nice to have in advance.

"We don't stand on ceremony around these parts. Please, Commander, call me Lois."

Lois—dammit, he'd already started calling her by her first name in his head—smiled and took his hand in a firm grip.

"Hank is fine, ma'am." Hank definitely did not need to be reminded he was her sons' commander.

She treated him to the same crooked smile he'd seen on both of her sons' faces so many times. "All right. Hank it is then. Maybe when you've been here a while we can lose that ma'am."

"Yes, ma'am." His face grew hot as her smile spread wider. Her eyes met and held his gaze before she withdrew the warmth of her hand from his grasp.

"And this big guy here is Bull." Jack moved on in the introductions, taking his mother with him.

"You sure are a tall drink of water. Aren't you, darlin'?" She looked up at him and smiled.

Lois moved down the line of guests, welcoming each, showing what Hank assumed was typical Southern hospitality. So why did it make Hank want to grab her and whisk her off alone somewhere where she'd call him *darlin'* and turn that brilliant smile on him and no one else?

"Y'all come on inside. We'll have some drinks and then eat an early supper." She spun and headed for the house, followed by the group of visitors.

Hank brought up the rear, trying to shake the tingle just hearing her voice and that sexy Southern drawl sent through him every time she spoke, no matter what she said.

He made a conscious effort to not notice the sway of her

ass in those jeans as she walked. He was in big trouble here. What he didn't know was what the hell to do about it.

CHAPTER FOUR

Matt leaned forward in his chair and rubbed his hands together. "What's on the agenda for the bachelor party, Jared?"

Every female in the room went still, waiting for Jared's answer.

Lois knew one thing—what happened at the bachelor party was best left at the bachelor party. "I'm afraid y'all will have to wait for that information. Jared, I need your help in the kitchen."

Jared didn't argue, but he didn't look happy. He followed her into the kitchen and frowned. "What's so important?"

"You not throwing a wrench into this wedding, that's what." Lois moved to the thirty-cup coffeemaker she'd borrowed from the church for the weekend and began to fill a serving carafe with steaming-hot coffee. "No woman wants to hear what her husband is going to be doing on his last night as a bachelor. I can guarantee you that a hormonal pregnant woman surely can't handle it. You want to brag about your plans to the boys, do it when the ladies aren't around. Understand me?"

"Yes, ma'am." Jared hated being reprimanded like a child. His scowl was enough to tell Lois that.

He'd get over it. Sometimes a mother had to do what a

mother had to do to keep the peace.

She'd worked too damn hard to make this event happen to risk it being ruined by an angry bride and a groom in the doghouse because of whatever shenanigans Jared had planned.

Lois handed the filled pot to Jared. "Now take this to the dining room. Cream and sugar are already out there. Come right back. I need help bringing in the pies."

"I can help." Hank Miller's deep and commanding voice from the doorway brought Lois's head around.

"Thanks, Commander." Jared sent her a smirk on the way out the door, as if he was getting away with something because of Hank's offer.

She couldn't deal with her son's behavior right now. Lois was too occupied trying to calm the racing of her heart. "Thank you, Hank, but you're a guest and that boy needs to be kept busy or he'll get himself into trouble."

"Ah, I see I've interfered with your plan. My apologies." He dipped his head in a small nod.

Mercy, he was sexy with that short silver hair. The muscles bulging beneath his tight black short-sleeve shirt didn't hurt either.

"No apology needed. I think I'll put Jared's girl on the case. Mandy'll have to keep him in line this weekend. I don't have the energy for all three of them home and the planning of a wedding at the same time. I'm not as young as I used to be."

She reached for a mug from the cabinet above her head and realized her hand shook. Dammit. She'd been without a man for so long, even being alone in a room with one had her trembling.

"Coffee?" she asked.

"Yes, please." A smile drew her attention to his mouth. "And if you don't mind me saying, you look plenty young to me. You sure they're really your boys?"

"Sometimes I have to wonder." She forced a laugh and handed him the mug, wondering if he was flirting or being polite. The second she could handle, the first she wasn't quite sure what to do with. Her flirting skills were woefully rusty. "Cream and sugar?"

"Black. Thanks."

Lois handed him the coffee and reached for a second mug that she filled for herself. Grabbing the container of cream on the counter, she sent Hank a glance as she poured a good amount into her cup. "I'm afraid I don't appreciate the raw flavor of coffee the way you do. I take mine light and sweet. Always have. My jeans would be far less tight if I could drink it black."

"I think your jeans look just fine the way they are." His lips twitched with a smile, before he raised the mug to hide them while taking another sip.

Wow. Definitely flirting. Lois swallowed away the dryness in her mouth.

Heart pounding, she met Hank's gaze. "Thank you. You're sweet."

"Nothing sweet about it. Just the truth." His eyes didn't waver as they held hers.

Phew. Maybe those drinks Carly had been mixing before supper had been stronger than Lois had thought.

She never would have guessed Hank could be this forward. Just as she'd never imagined she'd like it so much and want more. A lot more. Something she hadn't wanted from a man in a very long time.

Jared appeared in the doorway. "Mama. The pies?"

"Oh, goodness. Sorry. Go tell everyone I'll bring them right out."

Jared's gaze traveled from her to the commander as he raised one brow. "A'ight."

Her youngest had caught her blushing in the kitchen with a man like she was a teen. Lovely.

As Jared left them alone again, she let out a huff. She planted her mug on the counter and spun, about to head for the pie safe.

Hank's bulk blocked her way and she crashed into him.

As his hands came up to steady her, he said, "I'm sorry."

Good thing he'd put his mug down on the counter as well, or they'd both be covered in coffee thanks to her clumsiness.

"No, my fault." Lois did note neither of them had taken a step back.

They stood nose-to-nose with his hands wrapped around her arms.

Hank's throat worked as he swallowed. His gaze dropped to her mouth. "I think you'd better hand me a pie before . . ."

"Before what?" She reveled in the scent of him—something warm and rich and as tempting as the spices she'd put in the sweet-potato pie.

His nostrils flared as he took a step back. "Before those boys in there stage a rebellion."

She'd been out of the dating world for a long time, but Lois was sure of one thing. This man hadn't said what he'd been thinking. If there was one thing she was well-versed in after raising three Gordon men, it was to recognize when a man wasn't telling her the complete truth.

Hank was interested in more than pie.

The frightening thing was she wanted to give it to him.

CHAPTER FIVE

The women stayed behind at the farm for Lia's combination shower-bachelorette party while Hank, along with the rest of the men, left to check into some hotel in town named the Hideaway before the bachelor party began.

"Okay, Jared. Now we're alone, tell us the plan for the bachelor party." Standing in the hotel parking lot, Matt rubbed his hands together. "Any strippers?"

Bull cocked one brow. "I'm sure your new girlfriend would be interested in hearing you ask that. Better watch it, Matt. She's been trained to kill."

"Hey, I was interested for Jimmy, not for myself," Mat said.

Jack let out a laugh. "Well, nobody's girl has to worry about strippers. There ain't any in Pigeon Hollow. Not unless Jared imported some from elsewhere."

Jared cocked his head to one side. "Y'all will see. But to answer your question, Matt, the festivities will take place right next door at the bar."

Bull turned to look at the nearby building. "That's convenient. At least we won't have to drive."

"Very convenient. The one hotel in town is just a drunken stumble from the door of the only drinking establishment." Jimmy laughed. "I think that's what kept both places in business all these years."

"Y'all check in. I'm going to run next door and see to the preparations for tonight." Jared hooked a thumb in the direction of the bar.

It was getting to be full dark as the members of Task Force Zeta invaded the office of the Hideaway Motel as boldly as they infiltrated any assigned target.

After checking in with an overwhelmed-looking clerk who probably hadn't had this many guests at one time in his time working there, the men moved across the parking lot to the bar. It was then Hank got the first hint of what Jared had planned.

"Wet T-shirt Contest Tonight. Special Celebrity Judges," Jimmy read the sign hung on the door aloud. "Ah, crap."

"Oh crap is right, big brother." Jack broke into an amused grin. "Lia's gonna be madder than a wet hen when she hears about this."

"You're right here next to me, Jack. You think Nicki's gonna be any more understanding?" Jimmy grabbed the door handle and yanked. "I need to get inside and talk to our troublemaking little brother."

"I'm thinking you're all screwed as far as the women are concerned." Matt shook his head. "Me and the commander are the only ones safe from the wrath of the girlfriends tonight. Mine's OCONUS with Omega and the commander doesn't have one."

Hank ignored Matt's comment on his lack of a love life while Blake, holding the door open with one hand, hesitated and stared at the sign. "Who do you think the celebrity judges are?"

"No clue." BB shrugged. "We'll have to ask Jared."

A female screech from inside the dim bar cut through the air. Hank stiffened, on alert.

"Oh my God. BB Dalton!"

A mob of women, all wearing tight white T-shirts and led by the one who'd screamed over BB, pushed toward him.

"That answers the question of who the celebrity is. It's

you, dude." Matt laughed, getting jostled by a woman trying to thrust a pen and a cocktail napkin at BB.

The celebrity in question paled and took a step back.

Hank had seen Dalton fearlessly face arming explosives during a deep-water dive, yet these women had him in a retreat.

Without instruction, the team shifted into a protective circle around him. Like a well-oiled machine, they blocked the onslaught of scantily clad females from getting to their goal.

"Jesus, Dalton. Does this happen all the time?" Blake's eyes opened wide as he tried to block the path of one busty female intent on getting to BB.

"Only when there's a lot of women and plenty of booze," Matt answered for BB.

"Those damn ads are over a year old. I thought this shit would have stopped by now." Bull frowned down at the group of tittering females.

"Me too, Bull. Me too." BB shouted above the squeals. "Thank God Katie stayed at the farm with the baby. That's all I'd need is for her to be next door at the hotel, look out the window and see this."

"BB! Sign my chest." The girl whipped off her shirt and exposed herself to the world.

BB glanced at Hank. "Thanks a lot for giving me that assignment, Commander."

Hank couldn't rally too much sympathy for BB. The kid had been a pretty famous model in his own right before ever joining the military. And as far as team assignments went, having to pose for a few photos for the SpecOps recruiting campaign wasn't all that bad.

He shrugged. "We all have our crosses to bear, Dalton."

"Ladies. Ladies. BB will sign anything you want, but inside. Line up in front of the stage." Jared, the ringmaster of this circus, stood in the doorway, hands up as he tried to gain some semblance of order. "BB, go on inside. There's a table set up on the stage."

"I'm really one of the judges of this thing?" BB glanced at

the topless girl again before he yanked his gaze away. Hank would have found this even more amusing if Dalton didn't look so stricken and his wife wasn't in town and would probably hear about this mess from somebody.

"Could you judge?" Jared looked hopeful. "I had figured Bobby and I would be the celebrity judges because of Smalltown Heat, that reality show we were on last year, but you're a much bigger star than us apparently."

"Dalton, I suggest you get your ass inside and up on stage. You'll be safer and easier to protect." Bull glanced down as one woman, who didn't even come up to his chest, tried to get past him to BB. He turned and grabbed BB by the back of the T-shirt. "Come on."

With one arm extended like he was running for the end zone and BB was the football, Bull forged ahead. The rest of the team clustered around him acting as blockers. Bull definitely had a future in personal security whenever he retired from the military.

The team pushed through the hoard of overexcited and likely intoxicated women with BB in their center until they got to the stage. It wasn't exactly sanctuary, but at least he was above the fray and behind a table as the girls queued up on the floor in front of him.

The team looked more like concert security than party guests as they formed a line between the women and their end goal—a distraught BB.

Poor Dalton. Hank might have ordered him to be their recruiting poster boy, but it was the marketing team's idea to play up his past modeling career and run the Milano underwear ads too. And the head of that marketing team was BB's new wife, Katie. As far as Hank could see, he was blameless in the current mess.

"We gonna stand here and be his bodyguards all night?" Jack yelled over the din of country music and chattering girls.

It did indeed look as if Jimmy's bachelor party was going to be spent guarding BB.

"Things should settle down after they get their

autographs." At least, that's what Hank hoped.

"Yeah, his autograph on their tits." Blake watched another girl pull her shirt over her head. "Is this against the law?"

"In Pigeon Hollow? Good chance. There's a law you can ride a horse down Main Street, but you can also get thrown in jail for spitting on the sidewalk, so who knows? But the deputy is a good friend, so that should keep Jared out of jail." Jimmy glanced at the door. "Here's Deputy Sheriff Bobby Barton now."

A dark-haired man wearing a frown above his ice-blue stare moved their way. "Jimmy. Jack." He nodded to each in turn. "What the hell is going on?"

"Jared's idea of a bachelor party." Jack answered for both of them.

Bobby Barton, deputy, rolled his eyes. "I shoulda known."

Hank had begun to realize Jared really was the loose cannon in the family if even this decadent chaos didn't shock the law enforcement of a town as small as Pigeon Hollow.

"Ladies, we're going to start the contest here shortly. Make sure you get your numbers on your shirts and that your shirts are on." Jared jumped down off the stage and pushed past the crowd. "Hey, Bobby. What do you think? Pretty cool, huh? When we advertised the contest, I never thought we'd get such a big turnout."

"You advertised this?" Jimmy's eyes widened.

"Sure. How do you think we got so many girls? The bar owner ran ads on the local college radio station."

"I can say one thing for this idea of yours, at least there aren't any strippers for our girlfriends to get pissed about." Jack shrugged.

Hank cocked a brow as two girls got into a fight over their place in the line, until one ripped the other's T-shirt and the bartender came from behind the bar to break it up. "Nope, you're right, Jack. No strippers."

As far as bachelor parties went, Hank had experienced worse over the years, his own included. No, there weren't strippers for Jimmy, but thanks to Jared there were dozens of girls who would be as good as topless after their thin white T-shirts were drenched in water.

The girls calmed down after Jared began the contest, but Hank only sipped on one longneck bottle for the night.

He was drinking piss-warm beer, but he was sober in case all hell broke loose. He wished he could say the same for his men.

They were sucking down the alcohol while cheering for the show. Hank expected Jimmy to get drunk since it was his bachelor party. What he hadn't expected, but should have, was the rest of the team to follow suit.

Even BB, usually a non-drinker, was throwing them back from the stress of being a judge while women thrust their breasts at him.

Finally, the parade of girls in the competition ended, but the autograph line began again. BB refused to sign the naked tit shoved in his face, but he made the mistake of agreeing to sign the T-shirt for the girl instead. That meant every female in the competition lined up all over again for the same.

Hank shook his head and laughed. Poor Dalton.

Deputy Bobby had nursed the same bottle of beer all night as well. Hank could tell from the partially peeled label.

Good man. He would have made a good soldier.

Hank counted Bobby and the bartender as his only sober backup should the shit hit the fan, but so far, things had stayed relatively in check.

When the autographs were finally finished, Jared and poor abused BB joined the team.

Drunk though they were, protective instincts kicked in. The team shoved the new arrivals in close to the table and formed a ring around them with their chairs and bodies.

"You having fun, big brother?" Jared asked once he got settled in his seat.

Jimmy raised his beer. "Yes, I am. And the more I think about it, the more I realize that if Lia gets mad, I can just blame the whole thing on you. So thank you for that."

"Sure, bro. My gift to you." Jared lifted his own bottle in a salute. He'd just swallowed a mouthful of beer when his cell phone rang. As Jared glanced down at the caller ID an expression of fear replaced the cocky attitude. "Crap. It's Mandy. Shh! Everyone keep it down."

Hank snorted at that request.

The jukebox was blaring out a loud country tune and at least a dozen female voices were squealing closer by. Their little party of men keeping their voices down wouldn't do Jared much good.

"Hey, darlin'. How's the shower going?" Jared's attempt at sounding as if nothing was going on here at the bar came out sounding a little drunk and not so convincing as he slurred his words. He frowned and held the phone a little farther from his ear before saying, "It's just an innocent little contest, Mandy. I swear. How'd you even find out—No, you're right. It doesn't matter how you found out."

Jared cringed and then nodded.

"Okay, I'll be right home." He disconnected the call and glanced at his brothers. "I have to go home."

Jack and Jimmy broke out laughing but Bobby clamped a hand around Jared's forearm when he made a move to leave. "You can't drive. You've been drinking."

"I can take him home." Hank stood. He'd made an appearance for the bachelor party, supported the groom and his team, but now he'd had enough of being surrounded by girls his daughter's age. He glanced at Jack and Jimmy. "You two need a ride back to the farm?"

"No." Jared shook his head. "You two should stay. It's still early and your friends are here. No reason for all of us to have to leave. I'll go home and face the inquisition."

Jared offering to take the heat alone in a show of bravery was impressive.

Bobby held up the single empty bottle in front of him. The only one he'd had all night. "I'm sober. I can bring Jack and Jimmy home if they wanna stay longer. Besides, I think I might be responsible for Jared being in trouble."

"What?" Jared spun on Bobby.

"I told Christy about the contest when I called her before." Bobby cringed.

Jared's brows drew down in a frown. "You know your girlfriend is best friends with mine."

"I know. I never thought Mandy would get upset about it. Christy just laughed when I told her. Sorry."

"Too late now." Jared shook his head and then shot Hank a glance. "We'd better go."

"All right." Hank's gaze took in the rest of his team. They could walk next door to the hotel to get to their beds for the night. Hank didn't need to worry about them driving, only about them being here at this townie bar drunk. He looked to Bobby Barton. "You'll keep an eye on them for me?"

Even on leave, in Hank's mind they were still his boys. His responsibility. His to worry about. At least until they were back in their hotel rooms dealing with their own pissed-off girlfriends. Then, they were on their own.

"Will do." Bobby nodded. "Good luck back at the farm with Mandy and the rest of 'em."

"Yeah, thanks." Hank had a feeling both he and Jared might need a little luck and maybe a bucket of water to cool down the angry women.

Though seeing Lois again so soon certainly wouldn't be a hardship. Not after that heat he'd felt in her kitchen that had nothing to do with the oven.

CHAPTER SIX

Lois bent to retrieve the last few pieces of torn wrapping paper from the floor of the living room. She'd just shoved it into the garbage bag when she heard the ruckus coming from the kitchen.

The guests had gone home. The bride had been exhausted so she'd gone upstairs to bed while Mandy offered to wrap the last of the leftover food while she waited for Jared to get home.

Noise from the kitchen told her Jared had arrived. That would explain the yelling.

In between what sounded like Mandy railing on Jared, Lois heard the murmuring of male voices. All the boys must be home.

Lois set down the trash bag and headed for the kitchen to play referee to what she expected was going to be quite a battle between Mandy and her youngest about the bachelor party.

She sighed. She'd warned Jared not to plan anything too wild. As usual, he hadn't minded his mama.

In the kitchen Lois found Mandy, hands on hips, squaring off against Jared. His downcast eyes told Lois he realized he'd done something wrong, but it was the other man in the room who drew her attention.

Hank.

His gaze moved to Lois where she stood in the doorway. He sent her a nod before he focused back on Jared's girlfriend.

Lois drew in a long, deep breath.

This Yankee made her blood run a little too hot. She wasn't prepared for how her heart had sped the moment those steely gray eyes of his met hers.

She hadn't let a man into her heart or her life since the handsome, charming, seventeen-year-old James Gordon had gotten under her skin, and her skirt, when she was fifteen years old.

That relationship had given them their first son, Jimmy. Three babies and many years later, James's drinking, lazy, no-good ways had finally gotten to her. The time came to choose between losing the farm that had been in her family for three generations, or ridding herself of James and his gambling debt and raise the three boys alone. Lois did the sensible thing.

While Jared was still little, Lois had filed for divorce and hadn't looked back. But neither had she looked for another man—at least, not until Hank.

"A wet T-shirt contest? Seriously, Jared, what were you thinking? That it would be cheaper than hiring a stripper?"

"No. I knew you didn't want strippers there so I didn't get any." A deep frown creased Jared's forehead. "I thought you'd be happy."

"Happy?" Mandy's brows rose high. "That dozens of college co-eds were bouncing around practically topless? No, I'm not happy."

Jared shook his head, looking miserable. "But—"

"Lois, can you believe him?" Mandy cut Jared off and spun to face Lois.

"Oh, Mandy, I'm not about to get in the middle. This is between you and my son, darlin'." Lois would deal with Jared later. In private and in her own time and her own way. Though by the looks of things, he'd be punished enough by

Mandy he'd learn his lesson.

Hank literally stepped between them. Brave man, getting between a hellcat like Mandy and the cause of her displeasure.

"Listen. I was there and sober the entire time. None of the boys so much as touched any one of those girls. I give you my word on that."

The expression of gratitude on Jared's face at Hank's support was clear. The calm, soothing tenor of Hank's voice cut short any further ranting on Mandy's part. But the man's deep, slow words did the opposite of calming Lois. Hank set her pulse to pounding.

Mandy let out an angry sigh and crossed her arms, but she seemed to be out of ammunition, for now anyway.

Lois took advantage of the moment of silence. "You two go upstairs and get some sleep. Tomorrow's a big day. No more fighting tonight. Jared's had too much to drink to hear what you're saying anyway."

After a moment, Mandy nodded. "All right."

After one more deadly glare at Jared, she spun on one expensive-looking high-heeled pump and headed for the hallway.

"Thanks, Mama." Jared kissed Lois on the cheek and then glanced at Hank. "And thank you."

Hank responded with a nod.

Jared followed the path his angry girlfriend had taken, up the stairs leading to the bedroom where they would hopefully go to sleep, or make up. Lois didn't care which as long as they didn't argue all night long.

As the sound of Jared's boots faded, Lois turned to Hank. "Thank you for bringing him home and for keeping an eye on my boys."

"Not a problem. Two of the three are mine to take care of anyway. I left Deputy Barton with the team. He's the one who deserves thanks."

"I'll make sure to bake him something special and drop it off for him and his girlfriend."

"I'm sure that would be appreciated." Hank glanced

around the kitchen. "Looks like you're pretty much cleaned up here. Anything I can help you with?"

"I was just fixin' to bring the last bag of trash from the living room out to the bins when I heard Mandy squawking." Lois tilted her head toward the doorway.

"I can take it out for you." Hank moved toward the hall.

Lois jumped to follow. It was strange having a man around to do things like take out the trash. Jared was here, but he was so busy with the horses she handled the little things around the house herself.

She was sure there were a lot of things Hank could do for her—to her. Things no man had done in a very long time, and she wasn't thinking about his cleaning the ashes out of the fireplace or anything like that.

Hank and his long legs reached the living room first. By the time Lois passed through the doorway after him, he was standing over the cardboard box in the center of the room, peering down into the contents.

Oops. She'd forgotten all about that. She bit her lip and almost laughed at his expression when faced with a box filled with sex toys.

He looked up as she entered. "What kind of party was this?"

"Just your average bridal shower/bachelorette party. One of the women in my book club sells personal pleasure devices at home parties. Those there are her samples. She'll be by to pick them up in the morning. She had to leave the party early tonight to babysit her grandchild."

"Her grandchild." Hank looked a little horrified.

"Watch it. I'm about to be a grandmother now too, you know." Lois moved closer to Hank and the box. She picked up the plastic package her friend had given her as a thank you. "A grandmother who now owns a vibrator, apparently. This was my hostess gift from her for having the party."

Hank's eyes narrowed as he focused on the object in Lois's hand. He swallowed, sending his Adam's apple bobbing in his throat.

His gaze moved to her lips, then his steely eyes met hers. "I don't believe I've ever seen any grandmother, much less such an attractive one, holding a vibrator before."

Lois's heart pounded, sending her blood rushing through her veins until she got lightheaded.

They were standing close enough for her to see the beginnings of stubble on Hank's chin. Then her gaze moved to his mouth. She bit her bottom lip before bringing her gaze back to meet his.

Leaning in, Hank brushed his hand against her cheek, his lips temptingly close to hers. "Lois, if I'm about to make a fool of myself, stop me now."

She shook her head. "You are many things, Hank Miller. But a fool isn't one of them."

He thrust his hand beneath the hair at the nape of her neck, cradling her head as he crashed his lips into hers.

Blindly, Lois dropped the vibrator back into the box so she could touch Hank. She ran her hands over the bulging back muscles beneath his shirt. It's what she'd wanted to do since first seeing him get out of the car earlier that day.

Hank backed her up until her knees buckled at the edge of the sofa. She sat heavily and he followed her down, pressing her back into the cushions.

God, how she'd missed a man's weight on top of her and the feel of big, rough hands against her skin.

"Tell me to stop. If that's what you want you have to say it, because I'm not going to do it on my own." His voice was gruff and he sounded as breathless as she was.

His eyes mere slits as he looked at her, Lois could only imagine how she looked herself.

She felt the heat in her cheeks. She hoped he saw the desire in her eyes. "Don't stop."

Hank groaned as he took possession of her mouth again. When he slid his tongue between her lips, she welcomed him, invited him in deeper. A need long neglected surfaced as Hank thrust his tongue against hers.

When he broke away long enough for her to drag in a

breath, she said, "I haven't done this in a very long time."

They were tangled together like two teenagers necking in a car, and she couldn't care if she wasn't acting her age. It felt too good.

"Done what?" Breathless, Hank asked the question between kisses.

"Made out on the sofa . . . in this very room in fact." She laughed. "Tried to be quiet so not to wake anyone upstairs." Only back then she'd been worried about her parents hearing, not her son.

He moved his hands over her body. Every place he touched made her crave more. There were so many places she imagined his hands, his mouth . . . other parts of him.

Lois reached up and pulled him down onto her again. While he latched his mouth onto her throat, he ran one large palm up her ribcage to cup her breast. She pressed back against the pillow, concentrating on every sensation his touch sent through her.

Hank moved to brace himself on one knee between her thighs and connected with a place that had her drawing in a shuddering breath. He leaned closer, pressed harder against her and she gasped.

He pulled back enough she could see his face and his unfocused eyes. He took short, quick breaths and watched her as he slid a hand between them and rubbed.

The seam of her jeans pushed against parts long neglected and Lois's mouth opened on a gasp. He covered her mouth with his as he worked faster, harder with his hand. Her hips rose beneath him, angling toward the man who had torn down her long-held reserve.

The climax broke over her and she was grateful for his mouth over hers blocking the cry that remained strangled in her throat.

Hank broke the kiss and panted above her and she knew he needed more as much as she did.

Then the screen door in the kitchen slammed.

She heard the distant murmur of voices and her eyes

widened. "Jimmy and Jack are home."

With one hand against Hank's chest, she shoved him away just as Jimmy called out, "Mama? Where you at?"

All the lights on the first floor were on. It would be obvious to her boys she was around somewhere. They knew she wasn't the type to leave the lights lit and go to bed. She had to answer, but she preferred to be standing upright and not under Hank when she did.

While wiping one hand over his mouth, Hank shoved off the sofa and stood so she could too.

Panicked and still trembling from what they'd just done, Lois moved toward the doorway. "I'm in the living room."

Lois tried to smooth her hair enough both boys wouldn't know that she and Hank had spent the last quarter of an hour tangled together.

The boys looked good and drunk when they stumbled down the hallway and into the living room. That was fortunate. Maybe they wouldn't realize what they'd interrupted.

"Commander. You're here," Jimmy said.

Jack backhanded his brother's arm. "Told you I saw the vehicle parked outside."

"Yeah, I was just helping your mother finish straightening up around here." Hank bent and grabbed the trash bag.

"We can do that, Commander." Jack stepped forward to take it from him.

"I got it, Gordon." Hank held tight. "I promised your mom I'd take this out. It's the least I can do to thank her for the hospitality this weekend."

More likely it was because the stuffed black plastic bag provided much needed camouflage for the telltale bulge she knew firsthand was in Hank's trousers. Lois felt her cheeks heat at the knowledge she'd caused that reaction in this man.

"Thank you, Hank. I'll show you where the bin is." Ridiculous, but the thought of one more stolen moment with Hank for a private goodbye sent a flutter through Lois's stomach.

"See you in the morning, Commander." Jimmy nodded.

"Yes, you will. Goodnight, Jack. Jimmy." Hank returned the nod to both boys.

His promise had Lois's heart soaring. She and he had tomorrow . . . and tomorrow night.

Very aware of his presence close behind her, Lois led Hank out the back door and into the night.

The moon hung just over the treetops and, miracle of miracles, a cool breeze stirred in the summer heat. It ruffled Lois's hair and carried the scent of jasmine. She breathed deeply and took a second to absorb all the magic of this night.

The gravel on the driveway crunched beneath their shoes as they picked their way through the darkness, moving farther from the light on the corner of the house and toward the bins along the driveway.

Hank dropped the bag inside one then secured the cover before he turned toward her.

The moonlight fell across his face and her heartbeat kicked up a notch.

"I enjoyed tonight," he said.

Lois smiled, feeling sexy for the first time in a decade . . . and scared. "So did I."

That was an understatement. She'd more than enjoyed it. She craved more.

Hank stepped forward and reached out to cup her face between his hands. Her eyes drifted closed as he planted the briefest of kisses on her lips.

Groaning, he dropped his hold on her. "I have to go or I'll never want to. Good night, Lois."

"Good night, Hank."

"Oh, and make sure you get your hostess gift out of that box before your friend comes to take it." With that statement, so full of promise, he turned and disappeared into the night, leaving Lois with her pulse pounding and counting the hours until tomorrow.

CHAPTER SEVEN

Hank parked the team SUV in front of his room at the Hideaway. He glanced at the bar next door but didn't have it in him to walk over and make sure his men were safely in their beds.

That Deputy Barton had thought it safe to leave the bar to drive Jack and Jimmy to the farm made Hank assume the rest of his men had gone to their rooms.

With the taste of Lois so fresh in Hank's mind, he couldn't care too much about anything. That was a dangerous thing.

Lois wasn't the kind of woman a man could be with for one night. Besides her being the mother of two of his team, she was also a lady.

That's not to say he wouldn't take anything she was willing to give. Selfish man that he was, he wouldn't deny himself whatever time alone with her he could get. However much time that was, he had a feeling it wouldn't be enough.

He sighed and struggled to get his key into the lock in the dark.

Hank flipped on the light inside his room. It wasn't bad, just empty. Very empty, and he wasn't talking about the sparse furnishings.

Trey and Carly occupied the room next door. Hank could hear voices through the paper-thin wall. If they started having sex and he had to listen to it after what had just happened with Lois, he'd lose his mind.

After stripping out of the day's clothes, Hank made his way across the small bedroom, around the queen-size bed and into the tiny bathroom. He turned on the hot water in the shower full blast. The pounding of the spray on the tiles drowned out all other sound.

Maybe by the time he got finished, his neighbors would be asleep. He could only hope.

Eyes closed, he braced one arm on the tile wall and let the scalding water beat against his back. He'd wanted to plunge into Lois so badly tonight it hurt.

Hank could still see her in his mind, breathless and wanting.

He pictured her striding up to the box of sex toys and picking up the dildo and he was hard as a rock with no hope of sleeping tonight if he didn't do something about it. He reached for the soap and lathered his hand.

With his fingers wrapped around his length he stroked hard and fast. He imagined it was Lois's hand on him. Then her mouth as he tangled his hands in her thick, silky hair and plunged between her waiting lips.

That image did it, had his muscles clenching and his bare toes curling. Hank gripped harder and sped his stroke until he groaned with the release he sought.

Opening his eyes, he stared at the mint-green tile on the wall in front of him. He would give just about anything to have seen Lois instead.

He washed his short-cropped hair with the tiny bottle of hotel shampoo, soaped and rinsed the rest of his body and shut off the water. He'd shave in the morning before the ceremony.

One more day and night in Pigeon Hollow. No matter what did or didn't happen tomorrow between them before he left, he'd still have to go back to the base and his routine and forget all about Lois Gordon.

While sliding between the cool sheets, he imagined how

soft Lois's skin would have felt had he had the nerve to slip beneath her clothes and touch her tonight.

He had a bad feeling she wasn't going to be easy to forget.

Ignoring the renewed arousal between his legs, he flipped over onto his stomach. He punched the pillow into shape and then heard the rhythmic banging and soft moans through the wall.

Hank groaned for a very different reason than his neighbors. He covered his head with the pillow to drown out the torturous sounds, but the pillow couldn't smother his thoughts.

He tossed and turned for hours before he finally fell asleep.

CHAPTER EIGHT

The string quartet, Lia's father's influence, began the first strains of Pachelbel's "Canon in D" as the groomsmen rolled the white satin runner down the aisle between the rows of chairs.

The country band, Jimmy's choice, was set up under the tent for the reception later. The disparity in the music choices pretty much summed up the differences between the two families.

To further illustrate the dichotomy, on Lia's side of the aisle sat politicians, including the state senator and his wife, rich businessmen and the patriarchs of old Southern families whose names graced the state map for the towns named after them.

On Jimmy's side sat local townspeople, including the deputy sheriff and his family and girlfriend, Jimmy's teammates' dates and a few Gordon family relations and close friends.

There were close to seventy-five guests in all. Keeping the list even at that number had been a battle of epic proportions.

The governor had wanted to invite every political connection he had to the wedding. Lois suspected the only reason he'd given in and cut the list was because Jimmy and Lia had chosen to have it at the farm. Couldn't impress folks with a backyard tent wedding when the yard was attached to a working farm rather than a mansion.

Lois saw the expression on Jimmy's face as he watched the aisle for Lia's arrival, and realized all the dissimilarity in the world didn't matter. He loved Lia and she loved him, and that was enough. For Jimmy's sake and the sake of his new child, she prayed it would be enough.

From her position on the aisle of the front row, Lois was aware of the caterers setting out the hors d'oeuvres for after the ceremony. It was very unnerving having strangers in her kitchen.

It was all she could do to stay out of their way when they very politely suggested they could handle things and she should go outside and enjoy herself. Judging from the trays of tiny food she could see from her seat, she still wasn't convinced there would be enough to eat for all the guests.

The sun shone brightly as the uniform-clad groomsmen lined up next to Jimmy.

"That's one handsome group of men," Mandy whispered in the row behind Lois.

"There's just something about a man in uniform," Christy, Bobby Barton's girlfriend, agreed.

"Hey, I wear a uniform," Bobby bristled.

"Yes you do, sweetie."

Lois smiled at how Christy had soothed him, but she had to concur with the girls. The sight of the men, all in their various military dress uniforms, was breathtaking—BB and Trey in their Navy summer dress-white uniform, Matt, Bull and Hank in their Army service-blue uniform, and Jack and Jimmy in their USMC dress blues. Jared, the only civilian, was in a navy-blue suit but held his own amid the others.

Her gaze strayed to Hank once again. He was fine-looking in uniform—probably out of it too. That thought made her feel overly warm, and it had nothing to do with the sun overhead.

Lois tore her gaze away from the tempting man before he caught her staring. About to be a grandmother and she was at her son's wedding mentally undressing his commander. She was sure her mother, God rest her soul, would be properly appalled.

She caught Jimmy's eye and gave him an encouraging smile. He beamed back at her, happier than she'd seen him in a long time.

His expression softened as he stared past Lois and she knew Lia had come into view.

The music changed to the "Wedding March" and Lois stood and turned to face the aisle.

Lia walked behind her maid of honor—an old friend from home who'd arrived in town in time for the party last night.

Holding on to her father's arm and gazing ahead to her groom and her future, Lia looked more beautiful than ever.

That was the last thing Lois saw clearly. Her eyes filled with tears, and they continued right through the preacher saying, "You may kiss the bride."

The bride and groom did just that to the cheer led by the groomsmen and echoed, if more sedately, by the guests.

The wedding party led the way back down the aisle, although Lois was far too busy wiping her eyes to see. She was searching for another tissue in her purse when she felt a hand on her arm.

"May I escort the mother of the groom to the reception?"

She didn't need to look up to know it was Hank. A tearful half laugh escaped her. "Are you sure you want to be seen with me? I'm a mess."

He leaned in closer. "Happy tears make a woman more beautiful."

Her heart sped at the feel of his breath against her ear. "You're quite a liar, Hank Miller, but thank you anyway."

"I never lie." He brushed a thumb over her wet cheek then offered her his arm. "Shall we?"

Lois looked up and once again appreciated what a handsome man Hank was. She nodded.

"Oh and just a warning, the bride and groom get the first dance, but I intend on having the second dance with you."

Hank said it matter-of-factly and led the way to the reception.

Lois wasn't sure how she would be able to dance. It was all she could do to breathe when she was anywhere near this man.

CHAPTER NINE

Slow dancing with Lois as the sun set amid a blaze of color was very different than their first dance of the reception in broad daylight.

Hank wasn't even certain what they were doing could be called dancing. He rocked, shifting his weight from one foot to the other as he held her close.

Running his hands up and down the back of her dress, he felt the warmth of her body beneath the light fabric.

He shouldn't have pulled her so close. And when she rested her head on his shoulder, he shouldn't have laid his chin against her hair and inhaled the sweet scent of her. He paid for doing both when his body reacted to her closeness. He knew he was in trouble when he didn't force himself to move away.

They were pressed tightly together. She'd feel his arousal. That he wanted her to so she knew what she did to him proved Hank had lost his head over this woman. This off-limits woman who made him say and do things he shouldn't.

The song ended and he still didn't let her go. She raised her head and their eyes met.

"Lois . . ." He swallowed.

What the hell was he going to say? Come back to my motel room at the Hideaway? Real romantic.

Though it wasn't as if he could sneak away upstairs to her bed and hope no one noticed. Seven men trained to observe all, two of them her sons, would notice them running upstairs for a quickie.

There were too many problems with that scenario to even contemplate, not the biggest of which being Hank did not want a quickie with Lois. She was the kind of woman a man wanted to spend time with, both in and out of bed . . . and he was leaving tomorrow.

She waited as all these thoughts careened through his head.

Jimmy walked up to them with his bride and Hank dropped his hold on Lois and took a step back, angling his body behind hers so at least the bride and groom wouldn't notice his hard-on.

"Mama, Lia and I wanted to say good night and thank you. We're heading to the city with Lia's family in the limo." Jimmy grinned at Hank. "The governor is letting us use the presidential suite at the Hilton for the next couple of nights since we didn't have time to book a proper honeymoon."

"Very nice. Enjoy." Hank smiled, remembering how much Jimmy liked hotel suites.

"Love you." Lois teared up again as she kissed Jimmy and then Lia. "Love you both."

Hank knew Lois had said goodbye to Jimmy as he left for far more dangerous trips than his honeymoon, but he supposed this departure was different.

Her boy was embarking on a new life as a husband and a father. Hank could only imagine what he'd be like at his own daughter's wedding, whenever that time came. Hopefully not for a while yet.

Jimmy and Lia left, after a promise to be back in a few days to pick up all the gifts and spend some time with her.

Hank itched to pull Lois into his arms, but Jack had crossed the dance floor on his way toward them. He hugged his brother and new sister-in-law along the way and then came to Lois and Hank. "Mama. Commander. It's early still, so the rest of us are heading on over to the bar for some drinks. Y'all wanna come?"

"Thanks, Jack, but I think I'll stay here and see what the caterers have done to my kitchen," Lois answered.

"Commander? You coming?"

This was it. The moment of decision. Hank could agree to go to the bar, the last thing he wanted to do, but also the safest. Or, he could remain behind, alone in the house with Lois.

His heart pounded inside his ribcage. "Thanks, Jack. I think I'll help your mother clean up a bit and then head back to town. If you're still at the bar, I'll stop in."

Jack nodded. "A'ight. See you later. Night, Mama."

After a few more goodbyes, the last remaining guests were gone. Even the caterers had left. Hank and Lois were alone.

Lois paused just inside the kitchen door. She was nervous. Hank could feel it radiate off her. Hell, he was so nervous himself he was shaking.

"This house has been so full of people lately it's strange it's so silent now." She glanced up at his face.

He raised his hand and trailed it down her bare arm. "You must be exhausted. Would you rather I left so you can go to bed?"

"No. I'd rather you stayed so we can go to bed." She turned to face him and smoothed the chest of his dress uniform, concentrating on staring at the fabric, the buttons, his medals, everything but his face.

With one finger, Hank raised her chin so she had no choice but to look up. Her gaze skimmed his lips and finally rested on his eyes as he lowered his head toward hers.

With both hands splayed on his broad chest, Lois leaned into Hank's kiss. She undid the buttons on his jacket, slipped both arms under it and clasped them behind his back. He groaned and pulled her closer, kneading her waist through the fabric of her dress.

She parted her lips for his tongue and he was lost. He backed her up against the wall of the kitchen as he ran both his hands up her torso, brushing his thumbs over the sides of her breasts.

Her breath caught in her throat as she pulled away. "Hank . . ."

He took a step back, dropped his hold on her and ran his hands over his face. "I'm sorry."

"Sorry? No. Don't be. I just wanted to say we should go upstairs where it's more comfortable." She fisted her hands on each lapel of his jacket and pulled him toward her. "I know my mother wouldn't have approved, but I don't care. We don't have the time for flirtations."

She was right. Hank was leaving for the base tomorrow and the one thing he knew for sure was that he wanted to be with her tonight.

He brushed his thumb over her cheek and leaned in for another quick kiss. "Lead the way."

Upstairs, Hank concentrated on controlling his rapid breathing and heartbeat as Lois opened his shirt one button at a time. When she parted the fabric and lowered her mouth to his chest, he decided control was a lost cause. He wanted her, needed her, far too much.

She gasped as he picked her up and laid her on the bed. Had the staircase been wider, he might have been tempted to do a Rhett Butler imitation and carry Lois up the stairs.

Instead, they'd had to walk. It didn't matter how they'd arrived there, as long as they ended up exactly where they were— together in a room with a bed.

Hank slid out of his jacket, toed off his shoes and kneeled next to her on top of the quilt. Her skin was as soft as the silky material of her dress as he started at her ankles and moved his hands up her legs and under the hem to end at her thighs.

He was nervous. He hadn't been with anyone since his wife. He couldn't tell Lois that. It was complicated and this was not the time to bring up another woman.

How could he explain that after twenty years of marriage, they'd divorced and then continued for a year after the papers were signed to have more and better sex than they'd ever had during their marriage? Right up until the day he decided he couldn't inflict that torture on himself any longer and had made a clean break.

Now, she was remarried to her co-worker who—to quote his ex-wife—didn't routinely leave the country to try to get himself shot. Hank hadn't bothered to correct her and say he never tried to get himself shot. It just happened sometimes.

No, this wasn't the time for talking about the past. He wanted Lois undressed and under him. Spread wide as he thrust inside her. The problem was, he wasn't sure what she wanted.

"What's wrong?" Lois must have noticed his hesitation.

"I'm afraid I'm moving too fast for you."

Lois blew out a breath. "I was afraid you'd decided you didn't want me."

"No." He laughed. "That's not a problem. Not at all." How tight his pants had gotten in the crotch was visual evidence of that.

A small smile bowed her lips. "Then you aren't moving fast enough for my liking."

That was all Hank needed to hear. He slid his fingers beneath the elastic of her panties and pulled them down her tanned, toned legs.

As Lois's underwear landed on the floor, Hank appreciated the view.

He was contemplating his next course of action when Lois reached out and ran the tip of one finger over the bulge in his pants. If she continued stroking him, he'd come with his clothes still on and this encounter would be over much too soon.

He pulled his pelvis away from her. "We'll get done a little too fast if you keep that up."

"I guess you'd better distract me." Lois was no longer the quintessential Southern hostess. Not a mother or a grandmother or the baker of prize-winning pies.

She was all woman and she wanted him.

"That I can do." Hank slipped the hem of Lois's dress up and pulled it off over her head. She was filled out and well-rounded in all the places a woman should be.

Hank intended to show Lois his appreciation of her body with everything he had, beginning with his hands and mouth. He pushed the lace of her bra down and scraped his teeth across one pebbled nipple.

She shuddered beneath his touch.

While kissing his way over to give the other breast equal treatment, he slid one hand down her body. When he found the wet heat between her thighs, Lois moved her legs farther apart.

Hank accepted the invitation. He spread her with his fingers and found the tight bundle of nerves that made her gasp at his touch.

As he circled her with the tip of one finger, he brushed his lips against her ear. "Just so you know, after this first time, we're breaking out that vibrator."

She sucked in a sharp breath and raised her hips to press harder against his hand.

He slid a finger inside and her breath quickened.

Lois fisted the quilt as Hank doubled his efforts. She looked so beautiful, breathless and squirming beneath his hands. He watched her face, loving how she reacted to his every touch.

Her eyes closed as her breath sped. She cried out as she came with a body-shaking orgasm.

He didn't let up until she was a quivering mass on top of the covers. He was supposed to be distracting her, but he was the one distracted, clear out of his mind.

Lois opened those eyes that never failed to capture him, and he saw the expression of wonder in them. He ran his hands over her body and braced himself above her, wanting to sink his cock into her so badly he could barely control the urge.

In the dim light from the lamp across the room, he saw her face was flushed, her eyes unfocused as she whispered,

"You're overdressed."

He couldn't argue with that, so he corrected the situation. It would bring him one step closer to what he wanted.

His socks, pants and shirt landed next to her dress on the floor. He was usually more careful with his service uniform, hanging each piece up after he took it off even if it was headed right to the dry cleaner. Not tonight.

His briefs did nothing to hide the massive erection, but he kept them on anyway. Call it a security blanket.

He was in his forties but still nervous as hell about making love to a woman. It was ridiculous.

His only explanation—Lois was no ordinary woman.

CHAPTER TEN

Lois trembled half with the aftershocks of what Hank had done to her with only his hands, half with anticipation of what else he could do.

Hank stood next to the bed wearing white cotton briefs and nothing else, his body all lean muscles and hard angles.

There was one hard angle she'd like to get to know better.

"Come here, darlin'." She reached a hand out toward him.

He smiled and kneeled on the bed. "No one's ever called me that before. I like it."

"You're going to like this even more." Lois sat up and ran her tongue over the whorls of his ear. "Make love to me, darlin'."

"I can do that." Smiling, he tossed the briefs onto the growing pile of clothing on the floor.

Hank's muscles weren't just for show. While kissing her, he tumbled them back onto the bed and hoisted her on top of him.

Supporting her with two large hands on her hips, he lowered her onto his erection and then stopped.

"Shit." He pushed her off and cringed. "I'm so sorry."

"What's wrong?" Lois frowned.

His lips formed a tight line as he shook his head. "I'm not in the habit of carrying condoms. I was stupid. I should have gone to the store—"

"Is that all? Don't worry. I've got some." Lois couldn't help but grin at the shock on Hank's face.

She reached into the bedside drawer and pulled out a handful as his brows rose higher.

"Don't you dare start thinking what I know you're thinking, Hank Miller. Millie gave these out as favors at the party."

"Millie?" he asked.

"My friend who sells the sex toys."

"Ah, that's right. The grandmother with the box of dildos." Hank bit his lip and Lois could see he was trying not to laugh as he took in the colorful array in her hand. "So what shade are you in the mood for? Pink, purple or green," he asked.

"Hmm, well they're scented, so I guess that depends on if you want cotton candy, grape or apple."

He swallowed visibly and looked up at her. "Are they flavored too?"

"I guess we'll have to find out."

Hank drew in a deep breath at her answer. "Guess we will. Later."

He tore into the purple one and slid it on. Then he was over her.

Lois's leg rested on his thighs as he plunged inside with one firm move, sending tingles from the point of entry all the way up her spine until she could swear fireworks exploded behind her eyes.

He hovered above her, watching her face through every stroke of his body into hers.

Hank was a powerful man and every thrust moved Lois up the bed. He lifted her torso toward him and supported her weight in his hands. She wrapped her legs around his back as he knelt.

He held her close and stroked inside, once, twice, three times more before he let out a strangled groan and held deep.

Lois clung to him, neither of them moving for what

seemed like a long time while they both regained their breath.

She tried to move her legs from around him and felt how stiff and wobbly they were. She wasn't going anywhere. At least, not without help.

"Just when I thought I was in pretty good shape, I can't even move after a little sex."

Hank's laugh vibrated through her. "That was not just a *little* sex. But I wouldn't mind a little more. How many of those condoms you got?"

He made the tiniest movement, just a slight rotation of his hips beneath her, and she felt his cock growing hard within her once again.

She finally managed to answer his question. "About half a dozen."

"That might be enough." The look in his eyes told Lois he wasn't joking. Fully erect again, he swapped the used condom for a fresh one.

He scooped her up as if she weighed nothing and carried her across the room, sitting her on the big desk in front of the window.

Her eyes opened wide. "Hank, on my great grandfather's desk?"

"Don't fool yourself, sweetheart. I'm sure this isn't the first time this happened on this thing over the years. It's big and sturdy and the perfect height."

He rested each of her legs on his shoulders and plunged into her to demonstrate his point so convincingly, there was no way to argue it.

Hank worked her with his thumb while he loved her until she grasped at the well-worn wood along the edge. Every one of his strokes sent waves of pleasure through her.

He was working her toward another body rocking orgasm when he said, "So, where you got that vibrator stashed?"

His grin was positively evil and Lois knew after tonight she'd never look at this old desk the same way again.

CHAPTER ELEVEN

Lois opened her eyes as the morning light and memories of the night before swept over her.

Some days everything seemed right with the world. The sun shone, the birds sang, and she was sore in all the right places.

Her one regret was that she was alone. Hank had stayed as long as he dared, until the bar would be giving last call and her two boys and their dates would be on the way home.

Before leaving her, he had kissed her so thoroughly she hadn't wanted to let him go. That kiss made certain she couldn't fall asleep for quite a while.

It was a good thing he left when he did. Not ten minutes later, she heard the boys, along with Nicki and Mandy, trying to sneak up the stairs none too quietly.

She'd had sex with a man she hardly knew on most of the family heirlooms in the room and she was turning a blind eye to both Jack and Jared having their girls overnight in their bedrooms. No doubt about it, both her mother and her grandmother—great-grandma too—were not only rolling in their graves, Lois wouldn't be shocked if they popped right up out of them by now.

Glancing at the clock, she knew it was time to get out of bed.

The team and their dates, and most importantly Hank, would be at the farm for brunch in a little less than two hours. Then they would leave for the drive back to the base.

Hank was leaving too soon. She'd just found him and now he was going away. That was the only dark cloud darkening her joy, but it was a big one.

Most days Lois would wash her face, throw on some face cream and be out the door. This morning, she found herself staring into her reflection in the bathroom mirror, tempted to apply the full face of makeup she'd worn to the wedding simply because she'd be seeing Hank again.

She was in deep trouble. She was falling for Hank—no, she'd already fallen, as hard as hail on a tin roof.

Tearing herself away from the mirror, she pulled on jeans and a simple cotton shirt. She refused to change her normal routine over one night of sex.

Just as she wouldn't allow herself to miss him when he was gone or wonder what he was doing.

Right.

Lying to herself wasn't working, so she pushed all thought of saying goodbye to Hank out of her mind and jogged down the stairs.

She had to start the coffee and pull together brunch. Maybe she'd be able to use up some of yesterday's leftovers in addition to the frittata she had planned.

Good old Southern hospitality always did keep her mind occupied when all else failed to. Today, with Hank here for brunch while they were both under the watchful eyes of everyone near and dear to them she would need the distraction more than ever.

Jack arrived in the kitchen first. "Morning, Mama."

Lois shut the oven door and smiled at her middle son. "Morning, darlin'."

"You look like you're in a good mood." Usually oblivious to everything, Jack looked at her a little too closely today.

Lois busied herself at the coffeemaker and tried to seem casual. "Of course. What's there not to be happy about?"

"Morning. Coffee done yet?" Jared kissed her on the cheek and reached for a mug.

"Just done now." When she turned with the coffee carafe in hand, he frowned at her.

"Didn't you sleep well last night?"

"Why do you ask?" Lois took his cup and filled it, and then busied herself with wiping the coffee she'd spilled on the counter.

"You just look a little tired, is all." Jared continued to watch her.

She shrugged. "Big day yesterday."

"I guess." Jared took his coffee to the table and sat.

Jeez, when did her sons get so observant? Most days they wouldn't notice if she served breakfast with her hair on fire.

Thank goodness, Jimmy was already gone on his honeymoon or he'd be interrogating her too.

"Where are the girls?" Lois couldn't continue to feel paranoid and cook so she took matters into her own hands.

"Getting dressed."

"A proper gentleman would pour his lady a cup of coffee and bring it up to her."

Jared's brows rose. "Um. A'ight. Don't want anyone saying a Gordon man ain't treating his lady proper, now do we, Jack?"

"Guess not." Jack shot Lois a look and then took the mug Jared handed him. "Do I have to bring her breakfast in bed too, Mama?"

"No. But stay out of here until I call and tell you it's ready. I had my kitchen taken away from me yesterday by those caterers Lia's daddy paid for, but I'm taking it back today. So shoo, both of you, and don't come back until I tell you."

They sent her a few more strange looks, but finally she was alone.

Once she had the room back to herself, she headed to the pantry to grab more sugar to refill the bowl before company arrived.

She was just stretching to reach the canister on the shelf

above her head when someone grabbed her waist. She jumped.

"Mmm, good morning." Nuzzling close behind her, Hank kissed her neck.

"You scared me."

"I wouldn't think you'd be so tense after last night. I need to work on my relaxation technique." He turned her in his arms and grinning, slid his hands down her back to cup each jean-clad butt cheek.

"You're going to get us caught. People will be here any minute looking for food."

"Mmm, this is all I need." He nibbled on her lip.

Pressed against her the way he was, she had no problem feeling his need.

She knew she should pull away, but she didn't.

Up against the shelves of canned goods, she leaned her head back and enjoyed his kisses. She tried to memorize how his tongue tasted of toothpaste and he smelled of aftershave so she could revisit the memories later when he was gone and she was lonely.

These memories might have to last a very long time.

CHAPTER TWELVE

"Hello?" The youthful voice had Hank smiling.

"Hey there, pumpkin. How's my favorite girl doing?" He leaned back in his desk chair and let his eyes drift closed.

It had been a long day already and he still had a long night ahead of him. Hell, the whole week had been long.

A long, lonely, frustrating week.

"Daddy, you just caught me. I was on my way out the door."

He cracked an eyelid open and glanced at his watch. "It's twenty-two hundred hours."

"Yes. And?" She sighed. "Dad, I'm twenty-three years old. Jeez. Nobody my age goes out before ten on a weekend."

"At your age I was married to your mother and in the Army, and we already had you, so neither one of us was going out anywhere." Scowling, he decided to get back to the reason for the call. "I just called to say I love you."

"I love you too." Mary paused. "Daddy, is everything all right?"

Hank heard the concern in his daughter's voice. "Sure. Fine."

"You're going away someplace horrible, aren't you?"

He realized what being his daughter had cost her. "No, pumpkin. Just a training mission."

"At twenty-two hundred hours?"

He smiled as she turned his own words against him. "Night HALO jumps. Piece of cake, I swear."

"Daddy, high-altitude low-opening parachute jumps at night are so not a piece of cake."

He'd obviously over-shared with her when she was growing up. It made it hard to reassure her now.

Hank opened his mouth to comfort his daughter when there was a knock on his door.

"Hold on, Mary." He covered the mouthpiece on the phone before he said, "Come in."

The door opened and John Blake stuck his head in. "Sorry to disturb you, Commander. Coleman says to tell you we better roll out if we're going to make it to the airfield on time."

"Thanks, Blake. I'll be done in a second."

"Yes, sir."

Hank nodded his dismissal and waited for the door to close again. "I've got to go, pumpkin."

"Stay safe, Daddy." Mary's voice sounded so small, it took him back to when she'd been a child.

Every time he'd left for a deployment—or later in his career for a mission—saying goodbye to Mary would tear a piece of his heart out.

"I will. Don't worry about me. Say hi to your mother."

It never hurt to have all his ducks in a row before full-dark HALO jumps. Though there was one person he'd wanted to call and hadn't.

"I will. Good night, Daddy."

"Good night, pumpkin." Hank replaced the phone in its cradle on his desk. The desk in his office that held nothing personal. No family photos. No mementos.

Here, he was commander of the men of Special Task Force Zeta. Someone to be respected and sometimes feared. Sometimes a hard ass, always a leader.

He couldn't be those things and be human too. He didn't want his team to see him as a man with a failed marriage, a two-room bachelor apartment and a twenty-three-year-old daughter he still called *pumpkin*.

Nothing was here that belonged to Hank Miller the man, only to Hank Miller the commander and that's the way he wanted it . . . until that trip to Pigeon Hollow.

He'd thought he was okay with the way things were. That he was content being Commander Miller to the men, and Dad to Mary.

The problem was now *content* didn't feel good enough.

He wanted what he'd felt those few days with Lois. What he hadn't felt again since he'd said goodbye that morning after brunch.

But then what was the point? Until he retired, starting a long-distance relationship while on active duty and in command of Lois's sons would be lunacy.

And that was all he was going to let himself think about that tonight, because training or not, leaping from a plane at thirty-thousand feet required all of his concentration.

The desk chair scraped along the floor as Hank stood. He wouldn't let his team see him as a person, would never let them know he'd left a little piece of his heart and a whole lot of regret back in that farmhouse, but he would jump out of a plane on a dark, moonless night alongside these men.

He'd be damned before he'd let himself become one of those leaders who asked his team to do something he wasn't ready, willing and able to do himself. Any one of his men would give their lives for him without hesitation, as he would for them. That was what being a team was about.

Hank thought of his ex-wife and her new suit-wearing civilian husband as he strode toward the door and the men waiting for him.

Compared to a nine-to-five job, plummeting to the ground at a hundred and thirty miles per hour didn't seem so bad. In fact, he'd always found it to be a very freeing experience.

That, in a nutshell, was why there were men born to the call of duty and others born to sit behind a desk, answering phones and wearing a necktie all day.

Nope. There had never been any doubt in Hank's mind which kind of man he was.

That point was reinforced as his anticipation for this jump grew. His adrenaline began pumping the moment he and his team, minus Jimmy who was still on leave, pulled the SUV onto the airfield.

Hank suited up and pulled on the mask that would allow him to breathe one hundred percent oxygen while on the ground. That's when the reality of getting ready for a HALO jump squashed some of his enthusiasm, because as exhilarating as the jump itself, that's how boring the pre-jump preparations were.

The whole thing was a lot like Thanksgiving dinner—it seemed to take forever to get ready, and then it was all over quick as a wink.

But the hour-long pre-breathe rid the jumper's bloodstream of nitrogen to prevent the bends from being over thirty thousand feet up in a non-pressurized cabin.

Perhaps his ex was right when she had said his life was too extreme for her to deal with. Hank liked extreme.

The members of his team pulled out various reading materials and, in one case, a laptop, to kill the time. Looking at the guys, Hank hoped somebody had brought something along for him to read since he'd forgotten.

The oxygen mask made normal conversation impossible, so sitting around and chatting was out of the question and he was too keyed up to nap for an hour.

Hank rose to make his way over to Matt. He should have some kind of reading material to loan him. Though knowing the team's computer god, it would be some sort of technology magazine.

He was just reconsidering his decision and looking around to see who else he could bother, when a gray-haired man wearing a flight suit tapped him on the shoulder. Hank didn't recognize him, but he'd heard there was a new safety officer riding along with them tonight—not that his guys needed anyone to watch them.

There weren't any damn safety officers in the birds with his team when they were inserted into places most people had no idea American military personnel had ever stepped foot.

"I'm the safety officer on this one," the guy yelled to Hank through his mask.

The words were muffled, but Hank got the gist of it. He extended his hand and attempted to be cordial through the plastic barrier. "Nice to meet you."

Niceties complete, Hank turned away, about to go ask Matt for reading material, when he felt another tap.

The man shook his head and pointed a finger at Hank's chest. "No. I mean you can go home."

Hank frowned. "What?"

"I'm going up." He made a hand gesture to indicate *up* as if Hank wouldn't get the idea otherwise. "We don't need two of us for this team." The guy held up two fingers then pointed to the seated men.

Now he understood. The safety officer was so new he thought Hank was another instructor.

"I'm part of this team," he yelled back, pointing to himself, and then to his men with his thumb.

"Oh." The man's brows shot up and his eyes opened wider. "Sorry."

Oh? What the fuck did that comment mean? It wasn't just any *oh* either, but a distinctly judgmental sounding one.

Was this guy, who was no spring chicken himself, insinuating Hank was too old to be a member of this team?

All right, some of them were young, but Hank was only twelve years older than the most senior team member, Jimmy Gordon.

Frowning at the safety instructor's back as he walked away, Hank turned and stalked over to Matt. He slapped his shoulder harder than he meant to, startling him so he nearly dumped the laptop onto the floor. "You got anything to read?"

Hank wasn't in the mood for the *Sports Illustrated* Swimsuit Edition Matt handed him. He supposed he should be grateful it wasn't *Computer World* or something equally boring, but after the *oh* comment, even these sexy women weren't doing it for him. He glanced down at the bikini-clad sand-encrusted model and felt nothing.

Maybe he was old.

CHAPTER THIRTEEN

The next afternoon, Hank sat bouncing the rubber end of a pencil against his desktop while listening to the ringing of the phone through the handset.

It had been over a week since he'd left Pigeon Hollow and Lois.

He remembered how they'd parted. She'd fed the crowd and said the goodbyes. He'd gotten everyone and everything loaded into the vehicles, and then he'd run back into the house with the excuse of using the bathroom one last time before hitting the road.

Hidden away in the pantry, she'd kissed him as if it would be the last time. Then she'd donned her Southern-hostess smile and wished him a good drive, but he'd seen something else in her eyes. The same thing he felt. Regret that he was leaving.

Nine long days and nights of trying not to think of her and what they couldn't have, but after the encounter with the safety officer last night, Hank had reevaluated a few things.

The incessant ringing on the line was finally replaced by his daughter's voice. "Hello?"

"Hi, Pumpkin."

"Hi, Daddy. Sorry, my cell was buried at the bottom of my purse. So, um, how is everything?" His daughter always asked that question sounding reserved. As if she had to feel him out about what was happening because she knew he could never reveal details about where he went or why.

Hank sighed. It hadn't been easy being his daughter, but he was about to make things easier. He had no idea how she'd react so he tried to sound upbeat. "Everything is great. I have some news for you."

"Okay."

"Mary, I've . . . uh . . . met someone."

"Really?" Mary squeaked. "Oh my God, Daddy. I'm so happy for you. It's about time."

Hank let out the breath he'd been holding. "I'm glad you're pleased. I was a little worried how you'd react. It hasn't been that long since your mother and I broke up."

"Daddy. It's been almost three years and Mom's already gotten remarried. I want you to find someone of your own. So who is she? Where did you meet?"

"Her name is Lois and we met at a wedding I went to, but we can get to all that later. Don't you want to hear the other news?"

"I don't know. Is it good news or bad?"

Good question. Hank considered how he felt about it himself. It was a big change, but it was definitely good news, not bad. He hoped everyone else involved felt the same. "I've been offered another position."

"Um, okay." There was that wariness again.

"I'll kind of be taking a step back from the action. I'll be doing more training and recruiting. No more missions. Less travel."

"Oh, Daddy. That's great." Her relief was clear.

"Yeah, I think it'll be a good change." Hank hadn't always thought so.

When Central Command had been so impressed with the trainings he ran, and with his recruitment of Blake, they mentioned creating a permanent position for Hank doing just that for all the teams. Then, Hank had dug his heels in and sworn that he'd lead Zeta until they forced him out.

Now he saw things a little differently.

"Listen, pumpkin. I gotta go, but I'll call you soon."

"Okay, Daddy. Love you."

"Love you too."

"And Daddy, I'm really happy about all your news."

Her words made him smile.

"I'm glad. Talk soon." Hank disconnected and strode toward the meeting room. He found Jack and braced himself for the next step. "You ready to go?"

Jack grabbed the keys for the team vehicle. "Yeah, but I'm still not sure why we're driving two hours to see Jimmy at the farm when he and Lia will be back here at base in two days."

"The way you drive, it's nowhere near two hours, and as for why, you'll find out when we get there."

"Aw, come on, Commander. Not even a little hint?"

Hank had to laugh at Jack's persistence. "Has being annoying ever gotten you what you want from me in the past, Gordon?"

"No, sir." Jack's smirk never faltered, even as he shrugged. "Oh, well. At least I get to see Mama again. I wonder if she made pie."

"Blueberry."

Jack raised an eyebrow. "Sir?"

Shit. That had slipped out.

He couldn't let Jack know he'd called Lois. That he'd told her he wanted more. As much as she'd be willing to give him, if that's what she wanted too. That she'd said yes, she wanted much more.

"I . . . uh . . . called to tell Jimmy we were coming and he told me that your mother had picked blueberries and was making pie."

"I love her fresh blueberry pie. Wait until you taste it." Jack seemed far more concerned with pie than the details about the phone call to Jimmy Hank had never made.

Still, he'd be happier after he and Jack got to the farm and he'd made his announcement. Then there'd be no more lying.

He worried for the rest of the trip, right up until Jack

pulled the SUV up to the house. It was all he could do to not pull Lois into his arms when she stepped out of the door.

She hugged Jack and paused and said, “Hank. It’s good to see you again.”

It didn’t matter that he could see she’d stopped herself from hugging him too, because her smile beamed as she looked at him.

Hank smiled. “It’s really good to see you again.”

Jimmy came around the corner of the house. “Commander? Jack? I thought I saw the team vehicle. What are you doing here? Is everything all right at the base?”

Jack frowned and looked from Jimmy to Hank. “I thought y’all talked about us coming?”

Time for the truth.

Three sets of hazel eyes watched Hank—Jack, Jimmy and Lois.

“Do you think we could go inside and sit down together? Jared too. I have something to say.”

Jimmy’s mouth hung open for a second before he recovered. “I’ll go get Jared in the barn.”

“Um, I’ll go with you.” Brows raised, Jack followed his brother.

Once they were alone, the full glory of Lois’s smile lit her face. “Hi.”

“Hi.” Hank couldn’t help but grin back. He reached out and squeezed her fingers. “You sure about this? Once we tell them, it’s all out there.”

She nodded. “I’m sure. Are you sure?”

“Absolutely.” Hank let out a nervous breath. “I told Mary about you. She was thrilled. Now all we have to do is tell them.”

Lois glanced toward the barn. “Yup, and you’re doing the talking, darlin’.”

“You keep on calling me darlin’ like that and I’ll probably do anything you want.”

“I’ll keep that in mind.” Lois smiled.

The Gordon brothers were headed back from the barn.

Hank took a step back from Lois before the three boys joined them.

"Hank." Jared nodded to Hank and then glanced at his mother. "That pie done?"

"Um, yeah. That's a good idea. Let's all sit down in the kitchen. I don't see why we can't talk over some pie." Lois followed Jared in.

Inside the kitchen, Jared didn't sit. Instead, he leaned against the counter, arms crossed. "So, back again so soon, Hank?"

Hank ignored the cocky attitude and Jared's use of his first name. "I am. Couldn't stay away from your mama's pie."

That elicited a burst of a laugh from Jared. "I'm sure."

"Commander?" Jimmy shook his head. "I don't understand. What's going on?"

Enough stalling. Hank leaned his forearms on the table, very aware of Lois hovering somewhere behind him with a plate in each hand. "Jack, Jimmy. I wanted to talk to you two first because . . ." He drew in a deep breath and rushed to finish, "I'm leaving the team."

"What the fu—" Jack censored himself with a quick glance at his mother. "For real, sir?"

Jimmy seemed struck dumb. He didn't even thank his mother when she slid a plate with a slice of pie and a fork in front of him.

"Yeah." Hank nodded. "It's time."

"So you're just going to quit? Leave us? Just like that?" A frown creased Jack's brow as he pushed his own plate away from him untouched.

"No, Jack. I'm not going far. I'm taking a position training and recruiting for all the special task forces. I've got nothing left to teach you guys, but I can do some good with others. And there was another consideration." Hank glanced at Lois and smiled. "The new job means no more going wheels up on an hour's notice, or being out of the country for weeks or months at a time. It won't be nine to five, but it'll be as close to a normal schedule as I've ever had. That'll leave time for other things in my life. Jared, this part is for you too . . . I'm going to start dating your mother."

Jack and Jimmy had twin looks of shock on their faces, while Jared wore his usual smirk as he said, "It's about time."

His brothers turned to Jared, who looked from one to the other. "What? Don't tell me y'all didn't notice? They've been making eyes at each other since they met, and Mama's been walking around like a broken hearted schoolgirl for the past week."

Lois blushed. Hank reached out and took one of her hands. He squeezed it for encouragement then looked back at the boys. "I want your blessing, but I'll be honest with you. Even if you don't approve, I won't rest until I change your minds. I don't give up easily."

Jack snorted. "If you don't mind me saying, sir, that's a helluva understatement."

"You know, in a few weeks you won't be calling me sir anymore. You'll have a new commander."

"That don't matter. We'll always think of you as our commander."

"Thanks, Jimmy." What Hank didn't tell them was he'd contacted CentCom and recommended Jimmy, the most senior member of the team, as his replacement.

Jared pushed off the counter and headed for the door. "I think maybe Mama needs some time alone with her beau."

Hank nodded his thanks to Jared.

"I'll miss you in command, but I'm real glad the way things worked out." Jimmy stood. He bent and kissed his mother on the cheek before turning for the door.

"Me too." Jack stood as well, his pie plate and fork in one hand. "I'll be in the barn. Just give me a shout when—if—you're ready to go back. Of course, we could leave at zero-six-hundred and still get back in time for the team meeting. And I'll get to have tonight with Nicki. Your choice, Commander." Jack grinned and headed out the door.

"Could you stay the night?" Lois looked hopeful and tempting as hell.

Hank gathered her in his arms. "I guess I could. If there's somewhere for me to sleep, that is."

"Since it seems we weren't fooling Jared anyway, I don't see why you can't stay right here."

"I can't think of any place I'd rather be." Hank leaned in and kissed her the way he'd wanted to since he'd arrived.

Lois pulled back from his lips. "Tell me you didn't quit the team because of me."

"I didn't quit the team because of you."

She tipped her head to one side. "Now tell me the truth."

"Staying stateside and having more time to spend with you is just a fringe benefit. The truth is I'm forty-six years old. I took an informal poll. I'm at least three years older than the others in my position. During a HALO exercise, the safety officer assumed I was another instructor. He thought I was too old to be a part of the team, even as their commander."

"You're in as good a shape as any of the young guys and you know it. I sure know it."

He held her closer and raised an eyebrow. "Oh, do you?"

"I do. Although, my memory might need refreshing." Lois took on a devilish look.

Hank started backing them toward the staircase. "I think a refresher can be arranged."

EPILOGUE

Hank smiled down at Lois as the preacher said, "You may now kiss the bride."

He reached out and brushed the tears cascading down one cheek. She treated him to a watery smile. "Sorry."

"No apology needed." He leaned in and kissed her lips as the guests around them applauded and cheered.

Pulling back he extended one elbow to Lois. "Shall we go?"

She glanced at the friends and family surrounding them, all standing now as the bride, groom and wedding party made their way down the aisle between the chairs.

Lois stood and laid her hand on his arm. "Maybe by the time my last son gets married, I'll be able to stop crying during the ceremony."

His lips twitched. "Doubtful."

He led her down the white runner as a warm late autumn breeze ruffled her loose waves and blew the skirt of her sky blue mother-of-the-bride dress.

They reached the end of the aisle where the newlyweds Jared and Mandy stood, looking radiant as they waited to receive the best wishes of the guests queued up to congratulate them.

Jimmy and Jack stood next to their brother as groomsmen,

along with Bobby Barton as best man. Christy stood next to Bobby as maid of honor. The hugely pregnant Lia hung on Jimmy's arm, while Nicki flanked Jack on the other side.

Hank leaned in close to Jack. "You next?"

Jack lifted his brow. "Don't push, Commander."

Chuckling, Hank moved on. Some habits were hard to break. Jack and Jimmy calling him commander was one of them, in spite of the six months he'd been dating their mother.

He could only hope after tonight, they'd at least call him Hank. If Lois did agree to be his wife, he would never expect her grown sons to call him Dad—but he wouldn't object to it either.

"Mama." Jared hugged his mother close. "Why are you crying?"

Sobbing was more accurate during the ceremony. Now she'd gotten a bit of control back. Hank drew in a breath.

If she reacted this emotionally to her son's vows, he was in for some real waterworks when they said their own.

The real problem with that scenario would be if he teared up himself, which was a real possibility. Lois made him feel things he hadn't felt in a long time, if ever.

Commander Hank Miller shouldn't be crying in front of his men. But Hank, the man who loved Lois to distraction—it might be okay if he got a little misty-eyed at the altar.

But it would all be moot if he didn't propose.

Nerves weren't the delay. It was his crazy idea that he wanted the moment to be absolutely perfect—because that's what Lois deserved—that was the hold up.

A few more hugs and handshakes and he and Lois moved away to let the other guests greet the happy couple.

She glanced up at him. "I feel like I should check on the caterers in the kitchen. They plugged two coffee makers into one outlet and tripped the circuit this morning. If they did it again—"

"Okay. Let's go." With a firm hand on her back, he led her toward the house.

He wasn't about to let her start working in her kitchen in the midst of the catering crew that Mandy and Jared had paid a pretty penny to handle things. But Hank had an idea—another reason he wanted to get Lois in the house.

Inside, one of the staff assured Lois they'd moved the one coffee maker to an outlet in the pantry that was on a different circuit and all was well. He took that as his cue to move in.

"See. All is well." He laced his fingers through hers. "Come on."

When he started to pull her down the hallway, she tugged on his hand. "Wait. Where are we going?"

"Not far." He continued in the path to his goal—the living room.

When they arrived she glanced around the room, frowning.

It wasn't exactly as it had been the night he'd met her. Gone was the box of sex toys. In its place were stacks of empty glassware racks from the rental company.

It didn't matter what else was in the room, as long as Lois was there with him.

Drawing in a deep breath, Hank reached into his pocket, drew out the ring, and dropped down on one knee.

Lois's eyes popped wide. "Hank."

Her shock had him blowing out a short nervous laugh. "Lois . . ."

She pressed both of her hands over her nose and mouth, leaving only her hazel eyes showing as she watched him.

"I think I knew that first night we met that I wanted you to be a part of my life . . ." He laughed as hot tears burned behind his eyes. "Damn."

Time to wrap this up.

His throat tight, he could barely get the words out as he said, "Marry me?"

Her eyes shining, Lois nodded. She finally dropped her hands and said, "Yes."

Hank stood and pulled her tight against him. He couldn't get his mouth over hers fast enough. There in the room where so much had happened in so short a time, his future was sealed.

They had a few hurdles to get past still. He had to finish up his current contract and officially retire. That was a couple of years down the road.

He and Lois had been good at dating long distance so far. They'd have to figure out what their marriage would be like until he got out and moved to the farm, but they'd make it work. He had no doubt about that.

Hank forced himself to break the kiss and make this engagement official. He drew in and blew out a steadying breath and reached for her left hand.

Shaking more than he wanted to admit, he slipped the diamond ring over her finger and smiled at the sight of his ring on her hand. "Looks like we'll be the next wedding in this family, not Jack."

She latched her teeth onto her bottom lip. "Maybe not."

Hank frowned. "Hmm?"

"He came to me yesterday and asked if I still had my mother's wedding rings."

His eyes widened. "You think he's going to propose?"

She nodded, looking radiantly happy.

"Good. I want all your sons settled so you don't have a worry in the world except for making sure you're a happy bride and an even happier wife."

She cocked a brow high. "So I'm just going to be the little woman at home, happily baking?"

He let out a bark of a laugh. "Hey, I never said that. And believe me, I know that's not you. Well, except for the baking part." He grinned. "But seriously, I plan on devoting the rest of my life to making every part of your life as happy as I can make it. You deserve that and so much more."

Her bottom lip trembled and he cursed under his breath. His words were only making her cry. Time for action.

He leaned low and ran a thumb over her lower lip. Leaning in he hovered with his lips just shy of hers. He was going to have to wait a few hours for everyone to leave to do what he wanted to do to her upstairs. For now, this would have to do.

Pressing his lips to hers, he gathered her tightly against him and kissed her until they were both breathing a little heavy and he was wondering if they could take a quick tumble onto the sofa without the caterers walking in.

"Mama—Oh, Jesus. They're making out."

"Well, good God, Jack, don't watch."

Hank ignored Jack's outburst and Jimmy's response, but he did pull his lips away from Lois's. He leaned his forehead against hers. "Back to reality."

"Yeah."

He drew in a breath and turned to face the Gordon brothers. "Need your mother for something?"

Jack frowned. "I did but I'll be damned if I can remember what after seeing that."

"Get used to it, Gordon." Hank employed his commander's voice, but then softened. "It's going to happen a lot more often once we're married."

Jack's apparent shock was the perfect counter to Jimmy's grin.

"Don't tell me you didn't see this coming." Jimmy scowled at his brother before he stepped toward Hank, hand extended. "Congratulations, sir."

"Thanks, Jimmy."

He turned to Lois and hugged his mother. "I'm happy for you, Mama."

"Thanks, baby."

Jack stepped forward. "I'm happy too."

Hank lifted one brow. "You don't look it."

"That's because I don't know what the hell to call you now. Commander and sir aren't going to cut it anymore, but I don't think I can wrap my head around calling you Hank." Jack shook his head, looking pained.

"It's okay, son. We'll figure it out." If that was the biggest problem they had to get through, he and Lois would be good.

He glanced at her now. "I love you."

Her expression visibly crumbled at the words as her eyes filled again. "I love you too."

Realizing he was going to have to figure out a way to express himself without making her cry, he pulled her close and pressed a kiss to her mouth.

"Oh, jeez. More."

"Shut up, Jack."

By the time Hank looked up, it was to see Jimmy with a hand on Jack's back as they left, leaving him and Lois alone again in the living room. They'd have to rejoin the wedding party eventually but for now he was happy here, with her.

ABOUT THE AUTHOR

A top 10 *New York Times* bestselling author, Cat Johnson writes the *USA Today* bestselling Hot SEALs series, as well as contemporary romance featuring sexy alpha heroes who often wear cowboy or combat boots. Known for her creative marketing, Cat has sponsored bull-riding cowboys, used bologna to promote her romance novels, and owns a collection of camouflage and cowboy boots for book signings. She writes both full length and shorter works.

For more visit CatJohnson.net
Join the mailing list at catjohnson.net/news

Made in the USA
Middletown, DE
30 November 2018